THE
BETHLEHEM
INN *and Other Christmas Stories*

THE BETHLEHEM INN *and Other Christmas Stories*

by
FREDERICK M. MEEK

Decorations by Marian Ebert

THE WESTMINSTER PRESS
Philadelphia

BOOK DESIGN BY
DOROTHY ALDEN SMITH

Published by The Westminster Press ®
Philadelphia, Pennsylvania

PRINTED IN THE UNITED STATES OF AMERICA

Library of Congress Cataloging in Publication Data

Meek, Frederick M
    The Bethlehem Inn.

    I. Title.
PZ4.M4895Be [PS3563.E33]   813'.5'4   72-2029
ISBN 0-664-20943-2

For Sheila and Peter

CONTENTS

PREFACE

THE CHRISTMAS NARRATIVES of Matthew and Luke are at the heart of our recurring experience of Christmas, shared in by adults and children—indeed, by the whole Christian community. As Christmas draws near, the record is read and repeated and sung, times without number.

But there is a background to these narratives, a background of wondering and questioning—rarely spoken of or acknowledged—about people and events that are not mentioned. The wondering and the questioning can never be met by factual answers, for we do not have them.

Who was the innkeeper? Is he rightly to be blamed because there was "no room in the inn"? What of the Roman soldiers and the census takers who were in and around Bethlehem? What were the shepherds and the wise men like? How did they respond to the events of the child's birth, beyond the hints given in the New Testament tales? Were local Bethlehem folk in any way involved with Mary and Joseph and the child? What happened to Mary and Joseph as they traveled toward Bethlehem? How did they understand the birth of the child? What happened in Egypt? What were Mary's long thoughts? (She "kept all these things, and pondered them in her heart"—far beyond the day of the crucifixion.)

To play in imagination with these wonderings and their possible answers can create a further dimension of experience for all, young and old, to whom Christmas means joy and expectation.

THE BETHLEHEM INN AND OTHER CHRISTMAS STORIES gathers up some imaginative answers to just such wonderings. The details are not integrated into a consecutive unity, for, since the stories were written year by year, sometimes differing answers and differing sets of circumstances are suggested. Each story, however, focuses on the Christmas event.

In earlier days when our family members were younger, as Christmas Eve approached and a story was in the making I would try it out—perhaps of an evening while we were still around the dining room table. Their objective comments often kept me in line.

Since coming to Boston's Old South Church, each Christmas Eve I have read a telling of the Christmas story, as imagination, resting on the New Testament narrative, had pictured it for me. The service has become something of an institution.

My hope is that THE BETHLEHEM INN AND OTHER CHRISTMAS STORIES will be read in families, and at Christmas Eve and other Christmas services, so that by the reading, young and old will be helped to reach out and embrace the warmth and meaning of the birth of the Christ-child.

F.M.M.

Old South Church, Boston

THE
BETHLEHEM INN

THE
BETHLEHEM INN

WHEN SIMON went to live in Bethlehem he was sure that he was exchanging his turbulent life for the quiet and peace of life in an obscure Palestinian village. And for a time—nearly ten years—it seemed as if his expectation had found fulfillment.

Then came something different from anything that had ever happened in Simon's life, something different from anything that had ever happened to anyone in any community, anywhere. And because of it, Simon lost the peace in living that he had found, so that until near the end of his life he was more restless, more uncertain, than he had ever been in the danger-filled days of service with his Roman master, Fabius.

But Simon never left Bethlehem, because somehow he felt that there where he had found peace, and there where he had lost that peace, he might perhaps regain it. And he did . . .

And that finding is our story.

✦ ✦ ✦

Simon was black. Some folk, ignorant then as now, called him a descendant of Cain the murderer, the man whom, so these people said, God made the progenitor of the Negro race as a punishment for his evil deed. But such nonsense had no place in the thinking of Fabius, the Roman officer whom Simon had served from the time he was thirteen years of age. Over the years the lives of Fabius and Simon became closely knit, far more closely than one would ever have imagined.

✦ ✦ ✦

How Fabius first secured Simon as his slave, no one actually knew. Fabius, commander over all the Near East territory held by the occupying Roman army, had been away from Jerusalem on official duties since midwinter. When spring came, he returned to his headquarters in the city, bringing with him Simon, black Simon, to be with him and to serve him from day to day.

✦ ✦ ✦

Over the years Simon became more than a servant, and Fabius had an abiding affection for him. Fabius took deep satisfaction in shaping the lad's keen mind, teaching him the wisdom and schooling of the day—letters, figures, languages, astrology, and skill in arms. Between the ages of thirteen and twenty-five, Simon grew in strength of body and keenness of mind, until Fabius acknowledged (to himself alone) that Simon, Simon the slave, Simon the black, had outstripped him, Fabius the Roman. Simon became the principal agent for Fabius' affairs. For months on end he remained in Jerusalem and ordered and supervised Fabius' business and household while Fabius was away. And never did any man have a more faithful or a more competent representative.

✦ ✦ ✦

As the years passed, Fabius, wearied by his journeying and campaigning, began to take Simon with him as his constant companion. They traveled back and forth over the Near East, sometimes with shelter, sometimes without it. And they experienced the uncertainty and danger of traveling in countries where so many were hostile toward them.

There came a day when, on a back street, Fabius was attacked by three men who believed they had some fancied or real injustice against him. What the supposed injustice was is now no matter. The important thing for us is that Simon intervened. The sharp edge of the sword pierced the black skin instead of the white. But the blood that flowed was the same color, and the pain was felt just as deeply. The Roman physician at first despaired of saving Simon's life. But over the weeks, healing began and continued. It was clear that Simon's days of strenuous activity and travel were finished—at thirty years of age.

✦ ✦ ✦

Since Simon could no longer accompany him, Fabius felt that now he, Fabius, must be relieved of his command. He was called back to Rome to instruct his replacement.

Out of gratitude for seventeen years of faithful service, Fabius secured Simon's freedom—a free man! And then, before he left finally for Rome, he talked with Simon about what his future should be now that he was a free man. Simon spoke of his hope that perhaps he might settle in a community where he would be removed forever from the violence and uncertainty of his past military life. He wanted to be someplace where he would be with people, for he understood people and cared for them.

Fabius was acquainted with Bethlehem and its affairs. He was able to buy the Bethlehem Inn in the hill town, and he gave it to Simon, saying, "It is little enough, Simon, for saving my life."

There in Bethlehem, Simon lived and prospered, a free man. The people of Bethlehem came to accept Simon the innkeeper, Simon the black, as fellow citizen without let or hindrance, because of his understanding and warmth. And Simon the innkeeper became as well known as any man of his day all over the Bethlehem countryside. At long last he had found a home and peace.

Meanwhile, in Rome and in Palestine events were being shaped that were forever to change Simon's heart and mind—and life.

Word came that the emperor and his counselors had issued an edict calling for a compulsory census of men, money, and property in Palestine for taxation purposes. Always, this was done at the convenience of the conqueror and at the inconvenience of the subject people. Effort, substance, time—the expenditure of all these by people who could ill afford it was held to be of no consequence by those in authority.

✦ ✦ ✦

The legal period for taking the census was set for December. Thousands of families, traveling on foot or by the age-old slow motion of donkey, were on their way from where they lived to the appointed census areas in different parts of the country.

On the road to Bethlehem, journeying more slowly than their fellow travelers, were a man and a woman left far behind as others pushed on, seeking accommodations, which were bound to be limited. A passing glance made plain why this man and woman traveled so slowly. The woman, riding donkeyback, was "great with child," and her time had almost come. She felt that the slowness of their journeying must be burdensome to her husband. But as he walked beside her, one hand enfolded within both of hers, and the other hand balancing on his shoulder their bundle of provisions and clothes, his words of encouragement and his consideration allayed her fears and stilled her apprehensions.

What a contrast: Joseph, older than Mary, dark-complexioned, muscular, thick of neck and body, face lined and browned by wind and sun and rain, hands large, rough, marked by the toil of his carpenter's trade; Mary, slight, olive-skinned, misshapen with the weight of her child, dark-eyed like Palestinian skies at night. The strength, the understanding, the compassion, the affection of the man, as they showed themselves in his attention to Mary, were such that it was no wonder that years later their family life was to give their firstborn son a clue as to what God's nature was like, so that the lad called both Joseph and Jehovah the Creator, the God of Israel, by the same affectionate family name, "Father."

For Joseph, Mary was the fairest of women, a woman above all others, and, God willing, soon to be the child's mother. As they traveled, slowly and with difficulty, it seemed to him that Mary was deserving of something far better than this—traveling a dusty road seated on donkeyback; and much as he loved her, fit for something better even than bearing the burden of their child!

"Mary," his voice startled her in her pain and weariness, "see—there is Bethlehem, there on the hill."

She looked and nodded.

He could barely distinguish her words as she said, "Joseph, how soon will we be there?" And hesitantly she added, "These last miles I have been in pain."

"We will be there soon, Mary—before it is dusk."

And Joseph bestirred the lazy animal carrying the weight of both mother and child.

✦ ✦ ✦

Before dusk fell, they reached Bethlehem. The little town was filled with travelers. Joseph made inquiries of friends and kinfolk whom he met on the street, but there seemed to be no place where there might be a night's lodging. As they drew near the center of the village, there was the Bethlehem Inn. For hours, for long miles, Joseph had hoped against despair that somehow they might be able to lodge there. Leaving Mary, Joseph hurried to find the innkeeper.

"Sir, do you have room for my wife and me—even though it be just for this single night?"

"Look around you—look at the inn! Where do you think I could put you? People have been here all day, looking for rooms, and there are none. If you had expected accommodation, you should have come earlier."

And innkeeper Simon, who had had to make that same

answer many times that day, turned to other matters.

"But . . ." Joseph began—and when he looked up, Simon had gone.

Joseph walked slowly to the door of the inn. Outside, his eyes were drawn to Mary's lined face, and he knew that her pain was great. What could he do?

Joseph pushed aside his anger at the Romans responsible for Mary and himself being in Bethlehem, and in his desperation he approached a Roman soldier standing in front of the inn.

"Where is the innkeeper?" he asked. "He was in the inn a moment ago."

Joseph's desperation was evident to the soldier—Lucullus by name. Lucullus was new to the Roman military service, and he was moved by Joseph's despair.

"The innkeeper just went over to the stable to get his riding horse. You'll find him there. Ask him, man to man, to help you."

Joseph waited to talk with Mary before he hurried to the stable. There, Simon was standing at the door beside the stall where he kept his favorite horse. Joseph spoke impetuously. "Can't you do something for my wife? Her time has come! We did not think we would have to travel so near the day of the child's birth. What can I do? I must find a place where she can rest—somewhere—anywhere . . . where our child can be born."

Jew and Negro, there they stood, looking at each other. Simon's eyes fell.

"I can't give you anything. Can't you see the inn is full? The inn has never had so many people in it as it has tonight."

"But we have to find shelter! The night will be cold . . . and her pain is upon her."

For a moment neither man spoke. On impulse Simon turned and called to his stableboy. "Boy, take the horse outside—tie him and cover him with a blanket and leave him there."

The boy stared, wide-eyed. Simon cared for his horse even as he cared for a friend. "Outside? Tonight? Why—"

"Never mind that! And clean out the stall and bed it down with fresh straw."

He turned to Joseph as a man who understood, speaking to a man in need. "There! That's the best I can do for you. Bring your wife in here." And with that he was gone.

Joseph could hardly bring himself to tell Mary that this was the best he could do for her in her hour of pain and deliverance. But there was nothing for it except to bring her under the same roof as the cattle and the sheep, the oxen and the horses. As he lifted her down, he found that she was unable to stand. And so, gathering her weight into his arms, he brought her to the stable, to the stall of Simon's favorite horse, because "there was no room for them in the inn."

✦ ✦ ✦

It was time for the evening meal. But Joseph and Mary were not thinking of that. One of the servingwomen came across the courtyard to the stable, bringing food for them. She had been sent by Simon.

"How goes it with your wife, goodman?"

Joseph's breath came sharp with his own agony as he replied: "Oh, if only you could help! She needs a woman's care."

And with the innate sympathy of woman for woman in that strangely mingled hour of pain and triumph when new life is born, the servingwoman was on her knees beside Mary. She knew immediately that what Joseph had said was true. And thus it was that with the help of a servant girl, one whom men now call "Jesus Christ" was born, the son of Joseph and Mary.

✦ ✦ ✦

Simon could not sleep. The memory of the man and the woman and the new life in his stable disturbed his heart and mind. Slowly he dressed, came downstairs, and stepped outside to cross the courtyard. He stopped. Never had he seen a night so bright as this. What was this strange light that made the night as bright as day, even though the sun was long set? And who were these strangers gathered around the door of his stable—and the others inside? He pushed his way through, and he saw there in the stall that had sheltered his favorite horse the woman, seated on a rough stool, feet covered with straw for warmth. In her arms she held a child, asleep. And kneeling before them were shepherds, one or two of whom had once looked after Simon's flocks off in the distant hills.

"What do you here?" he asked.

"We came because we were told to come. We were told that in Bethlehem this night there would be born one in whose hands would rest the fate of all Israel and of the world. And coming, we have found it to be as we were told. And we have left these gifts." There before the mother and the child were the small tokens of the shepherds' devotion.

Before Simon could say how absurd it all was, he heard the commotion of new arrivals in the courtyard, the sound of men's voices speaking a foreign tongue, and the shuffle of camels' feet. As he turned, he saw entering through the low door of his stable, men arrayed in a magnificence such as he had seen only when he was at the far ends of the empire with Fabius. They too knelt in obeisance before the mother and the child; and they too left the tokens of their devotion—gold and frankincense and myrrh.

✦ ✦ ✦

On the morrow, because of a departing traveler, Simon had a room in the inn for Mary and Joseph and the child. And lest people should think him strange and question him, Simon made no mention of them.

When Mary and Joseph and the child were ready to leave the Bethlehem Inn, Simon bade them good-by and wished them well. "Nazareth," he said, "will be a good home for the lad."

"It may be," said Joseph, "but we go not to Nazareth. We go directly to Egypt, for we have been warned that we must not stay either in Bethlehem or in Nazareth."

And with the darkness of the night shielding them, they left the inn.

✦ ✦ ✦

After that night, there was ever a restlessness and a questioning at the heart of Simon's life. What was this that had happened in his own stable? What was the meaning of this amazing event? Always the question was with him, and never did he have an answer. But never again could he bring himself to shelter his dappled horse in that stall which had sheltered the woman and the child.

Once, months later, when he was out in the hills, he asked the chief shepherd what had happened that night. The shepherd said that he and the other shepherds went to Bethlehem because they had been told by an angel of the Lord that there was to be born there "a Savior, which is Christ the Lord."

From that day on, Simon pored over the Hebrew scriptures to see what light there might be in them to shed meaning on his perplexity.

✦ ✦ ✦

It was thirty-four years later. Simon was growing old and much of the detail of the management of the inn had been taken over by his eldest son, born to his wife Rebecca. But Simon was on hand to greet the guests, those who had been there before, and those who came for the first time. Rarely did a guest come once without being remembered by Simon should he return.

One night in that December, Simon watched a woman as she asked at the inn for accommodations. Slight, olive-skinned, clear-eyed—he knew that there had been a time when once before she had been a guest in his inn. With her was a much younger man, who watched over her as a son would watch over a mother.

Later that evening, as Simon stood in the courtyard looking up into the deep blue of the sky hung with the stars that were like silver lanterns in the Palestinian heavens, he saw the woman whom he had watched earlier in the day leave the inn, cross the courtyard, and enter through the stable door.

Why should she be out, going to the stable, in secret? He followed without sound. As he stood just inside the door, he saw her leaning against the walls of a stall, and with her hands she reached out to touch the rough boards, almost as if to caress them. It was the stall that for thirty-four years had gone unoccupied, the stall that had sheltered the woman and the child on that disturbing night. And then he knew! This was the mother. She had come back to the place where she had borne her son.

✦ ✦ ✦

Simon waited outside. As the woman stepped into the crisp evening air, Simon quietly said, "It was thirty-four years ago tonight, wasn't it?"

"Yes," she answered, without any surprise that he should know or that he should have remembered, "thirty-four years ago tonight."

"And where is your goodman?" asked Simon.

"Gone to be with his fathers these eighteen years."

"And where is the lad who was born here?"

"Did you not hear how he was killed—crucified—nearly a year ago in Jerusalem, at the time when they released Barabbas?"

He remembered that he had heard that story, but he had had no way of knowing that the teacher who was crucified was the child who had been born in his stable.

"Why was he killed?" Simon asked in wonder. And Mary, the proud mother to whom there had come the realization of the greatness of the child she had borne, told Simon about his life, his teaching, his death, and his triumphant living.

"I knew," said Simon, "that this was no ordinary birth.

But little did I know that the Savior of the house of Israel and of the world had been born here, under my roof. Tell me more of what he did and said and was!"

Mary answered: "There is far more than I could tell you, or would dare tell you. Why don't you go back to the inn and find John and speak with him?—John, who was nearest to him. John is waiting until I come back. He will tell you."

Simon walked back to the inn, where he found John even as Mary had said. But that night he found more than John. He found the Child—the Man—who became his Master and Lord. And in service to him, Simon was to find a peace far deeper than the peace that he had once lost.

In Bethlehem, thirty-four years after the first Christmas night, the innkeeper became a follower of the Way.

THE SOLDIER
AND THE CENSUS

THE SOLDIER
AND THE CENSUS

I T WAS near midnight. Marius, the captain of the
Roman soldiers in the Bethlehem area, was in his quar-
ters in the barracks. With him was his aide, Lucius. They
huddled close to the charcoal fire, for the chill of the December days had come. For a long time they sat without
words. Then Marius broke the silence. "I have been in
this country these last five years. I have served in Gaul
and in Spain. You can handle those people—but these
Jews who call themselves 'God's chosen' are a different
breed than any I have ever known. You don't get stabbed
in the back, you're not ambushed. The country is suppos-
edly at peace, and yet it is always at war with us. It isn't a
war of arms, it's a war fought by their attitudes. They
hate us Romans! When you pass them on the street, you
read it in their eyes. When a man strikes me, I know what
to do—I use my sword. But when a man looks murder at
me, I can't strike him down, because if I did, I would hear
about it from the commander in Jerusalem."

"I know," said Lucius. "I've seen it, I've felt it."

"And now there's this census that we've been ordered

corner under his roof in which to shelter your wife."

Joseph, leaving Mary, entered the front door. In a few moments he was back. He put his arm around Mary to sustain her, as in a taut voice he told her: "They say that all day people have been coming, and they've been told there's no room. I've got to find the innkeeper himself!"

Once again he turned toward Lucullus. "Where can I find the innkeeper?"

The warmth of compassion had not yet been disciplined out of Lucullus. He was remembering his own fear of mind and heart when his child had been born. He had wondered whether the child would live. He had wondered whether she who was his wife would live. And even though this man was a Jew—one of the subject people—it seemed that he *must* do something for him.

On impulse he said, "Wait." He walked across the courtyard behind the inn over to the large, sprawling stable. In the right-hand wing were the horses for the Roman soldiery. He pushed the door open and called out into the semidarkness, "Simon!" There was no answer.

These people, he thought, repeating to himself what he had so often been told, always take their time answering —as if they didn't hear. He called again: "Simon!" This time an answer came: "Yes—sir." The "sir" was delayed and reluctant, for Simon the Roman had become far more Jew than Roman in his years at the Bethlehem Inn. And he had come to rebel against the callous military authority that he himself had once represented.

"Come here!" When Simon appeared, Lucullus said, "I wonder . . ."—he could hardly get the words out—"if you would do something for me? Can you find shelter for that man and woman?" He pointed toward where they stood near the front of the inn. "Her time is nearly here,

34

and the child will be born before this night is past."

For the first time Simon looked the soldier full in the eye, as man to man. "You mean you want me to . . ."

"Yes, yes, that's what I want. I'll send them to you. You meet them here at the stable door."

Lucullus walked back to his post at the front of the inn. Joseph was standing there, just as he had been when the soldier had left him—eyes shut, body tensed, fighting against letting his desperation burst into sobbing, his arm still about Mary.

"Go to that far stable door," said the soldier. "You'll find Simon there. He may have a place where you can rest for the night. It won't be much, but it will be a roof." He paused. "And may the gods be with you."

✦ ✦ ✦

Joseph turned, hardly able to believe what he had heard. But before he could speak his thanks, the harsh voice of Marius broke in. "What's this? Are these people giving you trouble? Why have you left your post?"

"Sir, I was asking Simon if he could find a place for them to stay."

"That's none of your business. Let them stay wherever they can. Back to your post! In the morning report to Lucius, and I'll tell him to see that you're punished."

While Marius was disciplining the soldier, Joseph went to the stable door, and there he met Simon. It was there that Simon offered Joseph the stall of his favorite horse. At least it was shelter, and there would be some warmth, even if only the warmth that came from the bodies of the animals.

✦ ✦ ✦

When Lucullus went back to his post, he was elated rather than downcast. He felt that he would willingly take whatever punishment Lucius meted out, because he knew that the man and the woman and (the gods willing) the child were well.

His time of duty ended when midnight came. He was replaced by Servetus, the soldier who slept next to him in the barracks.

"Have you had any trouble?"

"No, it's all been quiet."

"That's strange—I've heard rumors that there will be trouble before this night is over."

"I don't think so."

"Well, if any comes my way, I'll know how to take care of it." And Servetus fingered his sword, while Lucullus, whose compassion and understanding had benefited both God and the race of men, walked back to the barracks.

✦ ✦ ✦

That evening every house in the little village was lighted, and lights shone from every window in the inn. But as Servetus was pacing back and forth, it seemed to him that he had never known such brightness. He told himself that it was because every lamp and candle in the whole village was lighted.

Marius stood at the door of the barracks, and looking across the fields, he was amazed—half afraid—for there was light abroad such as he had never known in Rome or Spain or Gaul, or here in Palestine. And overhead a star shone as no star he had ever seen. But it was for wise men and astrologers to tell the meanings of the stars. He turned to go inside, relieved that everything had been kept well in hand, with no more than the usual confusion and the usual pushing and shoving of the people into orderly lines. He began to feel that perhaps he would get through this cursed census without having to use any force.

+ + +

Inside the barracks Marius laid aside his breastplate, and dropping his sword beside his pallet, lay down to sleep. But sleep was long coming, for the light of the star seemed to creep in through every chink and crevice and to penetrate even his curtained windows. As he dozed, he was aroused by a pounding at his door. As he hastily dressed, he wondered who the intruder might be.

"Who is it? What do you want?" called Marius.

"Sir," said Servetus, "there's trouble. I don't know what, but there's trouble. When I saw that star, I knew that it meant no good. The astrologers will tell you that."

"I don't care about astrologers. What *is* the trouble?"

"Sir, people have been coming and going at the stable behind the inn. A half hour ago I saw camels leaving, and riding them were men who . . . who looked like kings. I've never seen anything like it."

"That," said Marius, "is foolishness! Who ever heard of men—kings—riding camels in Bethlehem? Have you been drinking?"

"No, sir. But, sir, I know what I've seen, and there are others who have come also, and they're still there. I had to report to you that things are happening—strange things that bode no good for us or for Rome."

"Why didn't you try to find out what it was before you came to see me?"

"I didn't know what to do, and . . . I was afraid . . . afraid of what this light meant. I *had* to come to tell *you*."

For a moment Marius was silent. "I'll see to it," he said.

As he cut across the field toward the streets of Bethlehem, it seemed to Marius that strange things *were* abroad. The night was filled with light almost like the day. And there before the stable were people—no noise, no commotion, but they seemed strangely excited.

✦ ✦ ✦

"What goes here?" Marius called, as he pushed his way inside. This was the stable he had always known; there were the cattle, and down the long dark corridor he could see the shadowy outlines of the Roman horses. Nearby was the stable dog. But what were those people doing near that stall—the stall in which Simon kept his favorite horse?

"What goes here?" he asked again.

No one answered. But the men pointed in the direction of the stall where that afternoon Simon had had his horse. Walking over, Marius saw that there in the stall, resting on a bed of straw, was a woman, little more than a girl, and in her arms a newborn child. Although her face was marked by the pain of recent birth, there was in it also beauty and contentment and peace, and a joy that seemed more than human. Beside the woman was the wife of the innkeeper, making her comfortable. Nearby was a man . . . Why, this was the fellow who had been talking to Lucullus that afternoon—the fellow who had drawn him away from his post of duty! And kneeling before the woman and the child, staff in hand, were shepherds from the hills. Marius knew them. He had often come across them when out riding late of an afternoon. How had they come here? Why had they left their sheep on the hills to come to see a child and this peasant girl?

"What are you doing here?" He shook the nearest shepherd's shoulder.

"Why, we came because the angel—"

"What do you mean—angel? You'd better tell me—or I'll know the reason!" He put his hand on his sword. But the shepherds were not intimidated.

"Yes," the shepherd went on, "while we were on the hills watching our flocks, the angel of the Lord came upon us, and we were afraid. But the angel said: 'Fear not . . . I bring you good tidings of great joy, which shall be to all people. For unto you is born this day in the city of David a Savior, which is Christ the Lord. And this shall be a sign unto you; ye shall find the babe, wrapped in swaddling clothes, lying in a manger.' And suddenly there was with the angel a multitude of the heavenly host praising God, and saying, 'Glory to God in the highest, and on earth peace, good will toward men.'

"We decided we would come to Bethlehem to see this thing which has come to pass—and we came. We ran all the way. We could because the light was bright as day, and, just as we were told, we found the child here in the manger."

The shepherd knelt again in the stillness. There was only the stirring of the cattle . . . and then the mother spoke softly to the child.

Marius remained standing, with his hand on his sword half out of the sheath. Suddenly the shepherd arose, wide-eyed. "Listen—you can hear the angels sing—now!"

And from far away, Marius heard the celestial choir: "Glory to God in the highest, and on earth peace, good will toward men!" And then all was quiet save for the dull click of a sword dropping back into its sheath as Marius left.

Returning to the barracks, he had no word to say to Lucius save, "If Lucullus reports to you tomorrow, tell him to be about his business." It was almost as if Marius were talking to himself. And because Lucius had never seen him so moved, he asked no questions.

✦ ✦ ✦

Whether or not the sight of what Marius had seen remained with him, we do not know. But he did see the Holy Child, and he did put aside his sword, even as the Child-Man had promised that all men would do in that day of peace which he foretold.

✦ ✦ ✦

A Babe was born that night whose spirit overcomes hate and bitterness. Herod is gone, the Child remains, and his peace is our salvation, and his promised good will is our surest defense and security.

"Glory to God in the highest, and on earth peace, good will toward men!"

MARY
AND THE
SEVEN BIRTHDAYS

MARY
AND THE
SEVEN BIRTHDAYS

I T WAS STRANGE that a woman in great pain should
have had the agony eased when from time to time she
caught the sound of distant singing voices. They sang as
no earthly choir had ever sung, not even in the Temple at
Jerusalem. The background for the melody sounded like
mighty winds whirling in great spaces. Even when there
seemed to be room for nothing else in her consciousness
but pain, the melody mingled with the agony of her travail. And as music and pain blended together, she seemed
to hear the words: "Unto you is born this night in the city
of David . . . the city of David . . . in the city of
David . . ." The words faded. "This is the city of David
. . . I am *in* the city of David . . . Bethlehem . . ."

The melody and the words grew loud again: "Glory to
God in the highest . . . For unto you is born this night
. . . born this night . . . born this night . . ." She realized she was saying the words over and over to herself.

And, there was Joseph standing beside her. "That's
right, Mary," he said, "born this night. You and the boy
are fine."

And Mary was asleep.

She was awakened by voices—insistent voices. Joseph reluctantly allowed the people to come in. They were shepherd folk, three men and a boy.

The older of the shepherds spoke no further word to Joseph but brushed by him and knelt before Mary and the child. "We heard the song," he said, "and we followed the star. We have come to you . . . to you and to your son, born this night, the One who shall redeem Israel, and, God willing, all mankind!"

Then, as if abashed by the forwardness of his act, the man laid down a lambskin. "Take it, and make of it a garment for him." The other man bent down to lay a staff beside the lambskin. "Let him have it for his own," he said. "It is the best of the three that I have. Jacob, the old shepherd in the hills, made it."

The little lad, son of the older shepherd, had watched it all with growing wonder. On impulse he darted forward. "I have this coin. Buy for him what he needs. I earned that coin as I watched sheep three nights in the cold for Nathaniel."

They stood, and having looked once more at the child, they went their way.

Mary reached out her hand to Joseph and bade him sit beside her. Both of them were perplexed by these strange things that had come to pass. "Joseph," she said, "they heard the singing too . . . as I did. I thought it wasn't real. But it was. And the voices sang for him—and us. What does it all mean?"

And Mary kept all these things and pondered them in her heart.

✦ ✦ ✦

School was not easy. It was hard for eight-year-old boys to sit cross-legged for hours on end, memorizing under an old man's direction. Often most of them didn't understand the things they memorized. And the old man had forgotten that eight-year-old boys are full of wriggles and turnings and sudden explosive movements of arms and legs.

The children, when released from school, were like birds set free from a cage. Shouting, leaping, pushing, pulling, they ran down Nazareth's little main street. There was a flock of pigeons in the road, impudent, like pigeons all over the world. Brown-eyed Bartholomew picked up a stone and threw it. Purely by chance the aim was good. One pigeon remained there on the ground.

A slight dark lad ran forward to pick up the pigeon. He held it in his hands. He ran his fingers over the back of its head. He held it near his mouth. It seemed as if he whispered to it. What the words were no one could say.

The wings moved. The eyes opened. The lad unfolded his fingers wher in the bird had been cradled. It stood, looked about, and then flew away.

The boys crowded around. "What did you do? What did you say?" But the lad had no answer beyond, "Oh, I told him the sky was blue, and the air was clear, and the tree-shade cool." The last to leave the lad before he turned toward his home at the end of the road was Bartholomew. Bartholomew turned quickly. "Thanks, Jesus." And he ran off.

That evening after Joseph had come home from the workshop, Mary was troubled. "Joseph," she asked, "why do they say strange things about our son?—that he is different—that he calls the dead back to life. He is just the same as the other boys. He runs faster than any of them. He is always chosen first when sides are picked. The boys love him. But Martha and Eunice and all the other mothers warn me that I must restrain him. Restrain him—when he is free as the birds of the air themselves, graceful as the sturdy branches of the trees, and loving as . . . as . . . *God himself!*"

"Wife, pay no attention to the gossip of idle women. They had much better be baking their bread and sweeping their floors than talking about our lad."

"Joseph," Mary asked, almost in a whisper, "do you remember? He was born eight years ago tonight."

And Mary kept all these things and pondered them in her heart.

✦ ✦ ✦

Joseph called the boy to him. "Lad, you have had your twelfth birthday, and you should come with us to Jerusalem for the Feast of the Passover. If we leave next Monday, we can be in Jerusalem on Thursday. There you will be in the city of our fathers and at the Temple."

So it happened that all that week the little family was busy with preparations for the journey. Eunice had agreed to look after those who were left behind. Mary baked and cleaned and patched and darned. Joseph worked longer hours in the shop.

All that week the boy played little. He read the parchments that contained the Law and the Prophets and the songs. His mother asked him, "Why are you so busy?"

"Because, Mother," he answered, "when I see them, I want to ask the rabbis and the doctors, 'Why?' "

"Lad, you will not get near enough to ask any questions. And besides, you are only . . . you will only be twelve."

The country boy found that Jerusalem and the Temple far exceeded his imagination. From early till late he explored all there was to be seen.

Mary and Joseph were unable to answer many of the questions that tumbled from his lips. "But I must know!" he said.

The Nazareth party left Jerusalem on Monday. Late Monday night, Mary and Joseph, who had met old friends, discovered that Jesus was not with the company of twelve-year-olds from his school. After an uneasy, restless night, they turned back at dawn to go to Jerusalem.

Where could he be? After three days of searching, they inquired at the Temple. And there they found him.

"Goodman," said the chief rabbi to Joseph, "this lad of yours knows the Books. Yesterday he besought me to answer his questions. We talked all the afternoon. At night I kept him in my home. And today—well, it is God's own truth, we have been asking him questions. He has the very wisdom of God in his heart. What a rabbi he would make! Bring him back, and we will put him in school under Gamaliel."

Three days later Mary and Joseph were talking of the journey. "But, Joseph," Mary said, "he knew more than they did. You yourself said that the rabbi told you so."

"Woman, let not your mother's love shape your judgment."

"But he did, Joseph. They were asking him, not he asking them. O Joseph, the wisdom of the God of Abraham, Isaac, and Jacob is in his heart and mind! What does it all mean?"

And Mary kept all these things and pondered them in her heart.

✦ ✦ ✦

Joseph had been ill these many months. The lad, with the help of James and Joses after school, was carrying the load of the carpenter shop.

As dusk fell, Joseph was in dire pain. Mary smoothed the pallet and gave him cool water. After a time the pain eased. Mary, silent, sat by the bed. Joseph watched her.

"Woman," he asked, "what have you on your heart?"

"Joseph, what kind of lad—of man—did I bear?"

"Why, Mary?"

"There are always intimations of something about him that I don't understand . . . Joseph, this is his sixteenth birthday."

"Yes, I know."

"I am so proud of him. He does a man's work. But I fear —for him—and for us!"

"What happened today?"

"I went to the shop with food for him. I stood watching. The sun came through the window and shone on him. He stooped to lift a great beam. As he spread his arms, his body and the beam made the shadow of a cross on the wall. It was as if he himself hung there, like Simon the rebel, whom the Romans crucified in Sepphoris. It couldn't be! It couldn't be, could it?"

"Calm yourself, woman. My illness has worn you out and tried both your heart and mind."

Mary thought little more of what she had seen, because the next day Joseph went to be with the God of his fathers.

Now she and Jesus were responsible for the family.

And not till long years after did Mary remember, but when she did, she kept the thing in her heart and pondered it.

✦ ✦ ✦

For almost nine years Jesus, as the eldest son, had been head of the household. The carpenter's shop had prospered. The folk of Nazareth discovered that nowhere else in the whole countryside could they get such fine yokes and plows, tables and stools and doors.

At the time of the midday meal, Mary came to the workshop.

When Jesus saw her in the doorway, he stopped to wipe the sweat from his forehead with the back of his hand and went over to greet her.

"Mother, what do you here, now?" he asked.

"Son, this is your birthday, your twenty-fifth birthday. What would you have me do for you?"

"It is not for me, Mother, that I would have you do anything," he answered, "but you can make this day live in memory if you will fill a basket full of food and come with me this night to the edge of the village. A little lad there is sick. The mother is a widow. Things go hard with them."

That evening Mary and Jesus went to the little house. Soon Mary found herself sharing her own experiences with Hannah. While they talked of what Hannah could do to provide bread for herself and for her crippled son, Jesus was talking with little Matthew as he lay on his bed, one of his legs sadly twisted and bent.

Hannah was saying: "Yes, but who will take care of my little Matthew? He cannot come with me while I work."

They heard an answering voice: "Oh, yes, I can, Mother! See, I walk as I did before I fell." They looked. The lad came across the rough floor with increasing confidence, walking with no trace of a limp.

"How? . . . Matthew!" Hannah gathered the boy into her arms.

Mary and Jesus left. They walked along the road, with no words between them.

As they drew near their own house, Mary said, "Son—where did this healing come from?"

"From God, Mother."

"Son, have you this power to channel the healing of God into crippled and diseased bodies?"

"It is no power of mine, Mother. I prayed for the lad. He prayed with me. And God healed."

And Mary kept all these things and pondered them in her heart.

✦ ✦ ✦

"Mother, for a long time you and I have talked of the time when I must leave, of the time when I shall be a carpenter no more. Tomorrow I am thirty. I think God wants me to go tomorrow. James and Joses and the others can help you. But I must go. It is a difficult time. Roman oppression grows harder. Men's hearts and minds are bewildered and perplexed. Oh, if only they would trust God more, as their Father, life would be so different! They could do so much more, both for themselves and for their enemies."

The next day, early in the morning, Jesus left home. Mary alone was up to bid him Godspeed.

The record of what he did in the following days is found in the Gospels and elsewhere in the New Testament—indeed, it is written in all history since that time.

But for Mary, who could not see as we now can, those days and months were a time of perplexity and doubt. Always she remembered his thirtieth birthday as an unhappy day, for it meant the separation of herself and her beloved son. For long months she never quite understood. Rumors came back to her. He had been here and there. He had done this or that wonderful thing. Then the character of the rumors began to change. She heard that Jews and Romans were raising their hands against him.

And all these things too Mary kept in her heart and pondered.

+ + +

One day a messenger came, tired and weary. He bade her go to Jerusalem. There she would find her son, who wished to see her.

She made the journey. But they never met until he looked down at her from the criminal's cross and commended her to the care of John—John, who later helped her to see and to understand.

Months passed. Many times the older women in Nazareth said to Mary: "I told you so. If only he had stayed home and worked at his father's bench! But he was ever one for overmuch study and for strange ideas. See what they did for him!"

Mary still pondered.

The chill of December came. Days followed each other slowly. Then came that night on which, thirty-four years before, Mary's eldest son had been born.

Once again they were saying strange things about him. Could they not leave his memory alone? They were saying that in Jerusalem men repeated a rumor that he was not in the tomb where they had laid him, and where she had thought him to be at rest and in peace.

Troubled, she slept. And she dreamed. She dreamed of the night of his birth. Once more she heard the sound of a melody such as human voices can never make. And the words: ". . . born this night in the city of David . . ."— they were the same. The words, the melody, and the pain were inextricably together, and she moved to ease the pain. She awoke. And she knew that it had been no dream, then or now. The angels had come to her on that first night of his birth, even as they had come to her now when he was no more with her.

But now there was a difference—there was no pain, only words and melody: ". . . unto you is born this night in the city of David . . ." And the voices swelled into full chorus: "Glory to God in the highest, and on earth peace, good will toward men!"

THE
LITTLE SHEPHERD

THE
LITTLE SHEPHERD

R EUBEN and Miriam and the lad Ephraim lived in one of the small shepherd huts clustered together in the hills nearly three miles beyond Bethlehem. Living beside them were Reuben's two brothers, Aaron and Joshua. And together the three men—Reuben, Aaron, and Joshua—shepherded the largest of all the flocks that grazed outside the Bethlehem village.

Ephraim, Reuben's son, was eight years old. He was straight and lithe in body, open-faced, resolute, and eager, and even as a boy he had the observant, far-seeing eye of the hill shepherd.

That morning Ephraim repeated again the request he had been making for many weeks now. "Mother, I'm old enough to go—I wouldn't be in the way, would I, Father? I could help—really I could!" The lad glanced from mother to father and then back to his mother, in eager pleading. "And, Mother, Father went for the first time when *he* was eight years old, just as I am now! He told me so, yesterday, when I asked him."

Confronted by that unanswerable argument, the

mother turned toward Reuben as she lifted her hands in silent protest. Reuben laughed and put his hand on Miriam's arm. "He won't come to any harm, Miriam. He has to begin sometime. We'll watch over him. Perhaps you'd better say yes this time." But wanting to keep her hold on her lad, even if only for a single day longer, she said, "Well, we'll let him go—tomorrow."

✦ ✦ ✦

Life could bring no deeper joy for Ephraim than to know that tomorrow, before dusk fell, he would be with his father and his two uncles, watching over the flocks by night in the fields. At the end of the day, Ephraim was slow to go to sleep. The anticipation of the adventure that awaited him stirred his mind as he tried to think himself into what would happen on the hillside fields, come tomorrow. When sleep finally came, it was as if he were nestled beside the warmth of the little orphaned lamb about which his father had told him.

Miriam too was sleepless for long hours because the yet unfulfilled promise of Ephraim's tomorrow brought mingled pride and fear to her mother's heart.

When morning came, it seemed to Ephraim, as he waited for the late afternoon, that the seconds were minutes and the minutes were hours. He was ready and waiting long, long before the men called him to go with them. His mother had clothed him warmly. She insisted that his father carry extra food. "Why, woman," Reuben said, "you give me enough food for the lad that would feed us all!" But he smiled warmly, for he understood her love and concern for their only son. As Miriam watched the three men—and Ephraim—stride away toward the fields, her eyelashes were wet, for Ephraim was taking a long step away from her and her protection into the kingdom of a boy's and a man's independence. And she knew that she could never go with him on that journey where, as a man-boy, he was beginning to share and to create his man's life.

✦ ✦ ✦

It seemed to the men that night that Ephraim was everywhere. Questions spilled over from his lips endlessly. And no matter how many questions he asked, there was his constant refrain: "What can I do to help now?"

After the first rounds among the flocks had been made, his father took him by the hand to where the orphaned lamb lay. "See," he said, "here is the lamb that is without its mother. We've been feeding it by hand. It's yours. You watch over it, help it grow, and bring it up, and the lamb can be the beginning of your own flock."

Ephraim's father had little of this world's goods, and gifts to Ephraim had been few: a toy or two whittled out by the shepherd's knife, his clothes, a few bright stones— these were all the things that Ephraim called his own. But now he had a lamb! It was his—something that lived and breathed belonged to him. His fingers wound their way through its soft wool. He fed it tenderly. Soon the boy and the lamb were asleep, finding warmth in each other even as the fire warmed them all.

✦ ✦ ✦

As the early hours of the night watches passed, the men tended the fire from time to time. Near midnight they too had fallen asleep or were dozing fitfully. Suddenly Reuben sat up, looking around in wondering perplexity. It was too early for the dawn, and yet it seemed as if dawn's light were coming, but coming faster than any dawn he had ever known. A full moon? No—these nights were the interval between the waned moon and the new moon. The whole countryside had become almost bright as day, yet without the day's illumination. His two brothers stirred, and as they shook sleep from their eyes, they were as bewildered as he.

"What is this? We've never seen it thus!" said Aaron.

"Hush!" cautioned Reuben. They heard the sound of many voices, rising and falling like the swirling, passing winds of a winter night. Then, near and clear, they could hear the sound. It was a chorus of many voices such as the ears of man had never heard before. The singing seemed to be just above them. The shepherds spoke no words as they felt both fear and wonder. A voice came, clear, strong, assuring:

"Fear not: for, behold, I bring you good tidings of great joy, which shall be to all people.

"For unto you is born this day in the city of David a Savior, which is Christ the Lord.

"And this shall be a sign unto you; Ye shall find the babe wrapped in swaddling clothes, lying in a manger."

Ephraim, wakened by the singing and the voices, watched and listened. No sound came from his lips, no move escaped his eyes. But as he watched his father and uncles, he saw that they were more startled than he.

The chorus swelled into its triumphant affirmation of praise and promise:

"Glory to God in the highest, and on earth peace, good will toward men!"

And then—silence—silence such as fell on a new world when God said: "Let there be light."

The eldest of the brothers, Aaron, whispered, "What can it mean?"

Reuben, a true son of Israel, answered: "This is what the prophets have long foretold; the birth of him who is to save Israel. 'Let us now go even unto Bethlehem, and see this thing which is come to pass, which the Lord hath made known unto us.'"

Slowly the men lifted themselves to their feet, their sheep and even Ephraim forgotten in the wonder of what they had seen and heard.

"Ah, but we have nothing to take to the child, to the promised Holy One. How can we go to him who is to save Israel without some tokens of our devotion?"

"True," said Reuben, "but we must take what we have . . ." He bent down. "Here is my shepherd's staff. It is a good staff. The Savior of Israel will know about sheep. His people have long shepherded them. Yes, and Aaron's water bag . . . we can take that. And this shawl—it has kept me warm on the coldest nights."

"Let us go."

And without further word they were on their way.

✦ ✦ ✦

Ephraim remained lying before the fire. He realized that the men had forgotten that he had come with them that night. He knew, too, that they were going to see a child "wrapped in swaddling clothes," a child that had something to do with Israel and with the Lord God. Why, this might be the Messiah about whom his mother had told him, the Holy One of Israel about whom he had

59

learned from the rabbi! Well, if his father and uncles were going, he was going too . . . But what could *he* take as *his* gift? In an impulse of affectionate understanding, he lifted the lamb—his own lamb—into his arms. This would be his gift for the child. And Ephraim too was on his way to Bethlehem to see this thing which had come to pass, which the Lord had made known.

How Ephraim kept within seeing distance of his hurrying father and uncles, no one could ever understand. Burdened with the weight of the lamb in his arms, his legs tired until they ached and throbbed, his breath came in gasping sobs. But he ran, and walked, and walked, and ran.

✦ ✦ ✦

When the three shepherds reached Bethlehem, they saw that the star stood directly over the stable behind the inn. As they drew near the stable, they waited outside for some time, trying to decide what they should do and say. As they were talking, they heard a panting, sobbing voice: "Wait! Wait! Wait for me!" Startled, they saw Ephraim, his face wet with tears and grime and sweat, stumbling down over the rough incline and coming toward them. Reuben drew in his breath sharply as he said: "Why, Ephraim!—we had forgotten you! How did you come here?"

"I came—I wanted—I wanted to see—the child too!"

"What is that in your arms?" And in amazed wonder they saw that it was the lamb which had been given to the boy.

"How did you ever manage to carry it with you, Ephraim?" asked his father kindly.

"I don't know," said Ephraim, "but I brought it so that I could give it to him as my gift. You have your gifts, and this is mine."

"I'll never understand it, lad," said Reuben.

They knocked at the stable door. Joseph, expecting no visitors, was puzzled as he called out through the slight opening, "Who is it?"

"We have been told of the birth of the child—the angels sang—one of them spoke to us, and he said that we would find the child wrapped in swaddling clothes in the manger. And we have brought him gifts."

"There are wondrously strange things this night," said Joseph as he opened the door. And then it was as if he were talking to himself: "Even when, months ago, the messenger of the Lord told me that I must not put her away—Mary—I never dreamed that it would be like this —the voices, the light—and the contentment upon her face." He lifted his eyes—the shepherds were waiting. "Come in and see what you would."

The men and the boy entered the stable. Never had they, or any others, seen a mother and a child such as these two, because the warmth of the hand of God was still upon the child and the mother.

The shepherds knelt and laid their gifts beside the manger. "These were all we had," said Reuben, "but we brought them for him." And Ephraim, with his eyes fixed on the child, crossed the straw-covered floor to lay his lamb next to the other gifts. He turned to Joseph. "It's mine, and it's for him. Will you take care of it for him until he can care for it by himself?"

And it seemed as if the child in the manger smiled.

✦ ✦ ✦

Dawn was breaking as the men and the boy walked back to the forgotten sheep. They fumbled in vain as they sought for words to describe and to recall the wonder of what they had seen and heard and done.

But the glory of God was in their hearts, a glory that was to remain with them all their days.

✦ ✦ ✦

It seemed strange to Mary that along with the gold and frankincense and myrrh which the wise men later brought, and along with the staff and the water bottle and the shawl, there should be a lamb.

When the little family left hurriedly to go to Egypt, practical Joseph offered the lamb to Simon the innkeeper to help pay for their stay in the stable. But before they began the journey, Simon came to Joseph. "You can't leave the lamb behind—it's the child's. Take it with you. I can't tell you why, but I know that you must take it and watch over it. It was the gift of the little shepherd." And this is how the gift of the little shepherd went with Mary and Joseph and the child to Egypt.

✦ ✦ ✦

In Egypt the lamb grew side by side with the child. When finally they came back from Egypt to Nazareth, the lamb became the first of the small flock of sheep owned and cared for by Joseph and the family. As Jesus grew into boyhood, the flock became his especial care. Sometimes he would say to his mother and father that he wondered at the stupidity of sheep—how that when he wanted the best for them, they seemed intent on finding the worst—how easily they were led out of the safety of the fold by a sheep that seemed to prefer danger. But he cared for them and loved them!

✦ ✦ ✦

The wool that was sheared each year from the little flock was the finest in texture and the heaviest in weight in the whole area. There was something more than ordinary about the flock begun for the child by Ephraim.

Joseph died, and with the breadwinner gone, Mary and Jesus and the family were often in dire need.

There came a day when Jesus said to Mary: "Mother, last night at supper our bowls were full; yours was almost empty. Was that all the food there was in the house?" Mary nodded assent. "Mother, you cannot deny yourself for us. We can sell—we can sell the sheep."

The next day the lad Jesus stopped some merchants who were passing through the streets of Nazareth. "Would you like to buy the finest sheep in this whole countryside?" he asked. The men smiled. "See!" said Jesus. And there behind him was the sheep that had once been left him by the little shepherd.

The men looked guardedly and questioningly at each other, for never had they seen such finely textured white wool. "Are the others like this one?" they asked.

"Almost as good," said Jesus.

Later that day, and for long after, there was money for food. And that night Mary's bowl was full even as were those of the others.

The sheep were given over to a new shepherd. He did not understand them as well as the boy shepherd in Nazareth, but he cared for them well because the sheep meant a profit to those who owned them. No garments were so soft, no garments were so long-wearing, as those made from the wool from this flock, begun by the gift of the little shepherd to him who was to be the Shepherd of the world.

+ + +

Years passed. Jesus became a controversial figure in the life of Israel, a controversial figure in the life of all mankind.

In Jerusalem a centurion's son was ill—ill nigh unto death. The centurion sent his emissaries to see if this Jewish teacher, this creator of turmoil against the authorities whom the centurion himself represented, would heal his son. Jesus healed the boy, and the boy found new life. Always the centurion was grateful—grateful and uneasy. In his own heart he became a follower. Never was he able to persuade Jesus to accept the gift of money that he offered to him in gratitude.

One day as the centurion walked through the marketplace he saw in a merchant's display a garment such as he had never seen before—a cloak, white, spotless, whole, without seam, made from the finest wool. "That," thought the centurion, "shall be his." He could not know that the garment was made from the wool of the flock that began when the little shepherd visited the child on his birthnight. But for the rest of his ministry Jesus wore the seamless robe. And this was the garment for which the soldiers cast lots rather than divide it when they gambled for it in the shadow of the cross.

+ + +

After the cross came the resurrection. And then there was that day when Jesus spoke his final words to those who had companioned with him. Even though his life now had the character of eternity, he recalled the days that he had spent with his sheep, for he said to Peter, "Feed my sheep." And he said it again and again.

THEY SEE,
BUT THEY DO NOT
UNDERSTAND

THEY SEE,
BUT THEY DO NOT
UNDERSTAND

ONLY THOSE who have known at first hand the oppression of life lived under a ruling alien power can really understand the uneasiness and fear that pervade such living. From hour to hour, from day to day, there is fear of the unknown "they" who in those distant places of power can let live or command death. At any hour of the day or night, the whim of an official, set forth in a written order or in an offhand spoken word, evicts a person from home or village, confiscates property, separates families, brings imprisonment or a killing. The life of men and women ruled by an alien power accountable to no law save its own well-being and affluence is precarious and hard.

And two thousand years ago life in Palestine under Roman rule was lived under just such fear and uncertainty.

✦ ✦ ✦

It was the day after the Sabbath. Joseph had left home early to buy rough lumber and fine cedar for his carpenter shop. The cedar he wanted was becoming scarce, but Naaman the wood merchant had finally found what Joseph needed. As Joseph reached for his moneybag, Naaman burst out: "I've been wanting to ask you—Where do you have to go to register for this new tax? As if we didn't have taxes enough! And more taxes mean more legions to hold us down—'to keep order' is what they call it."

"Register? What do you mean?" Joseph asked.

"Why, don't you know? Caesar Augustus' orders are that every one of us Hebrews has to go to his native city to register before the end of December." Indignation fired Naaman as he spoke and he trembled in hot anger. "It's easy to sit in Rome and order people like us shoved around. They've never seen us, they despise us . . . Can't they imagine, just for once, what happens to us? I've got a business. I can't walk out of here, just at their say-so—I'll lose money. If I had my way, I'd . . ." His loud, shrill voice trailed off into apprehensive silence. "Joseph," Naaman begged, "you won't tell anyone how I feel about this, will you? Promise?—the local Roman camp buys its supplies from me. And if they heard—I'd be out of business."

"I won't say anything . . . How much did you say I owe you?" asked Joseph. He counted out the money, and like a man in a trance, he loaded the donkeys and then turned his face homeward. As he walked beside the animals, he guided them by the unconscious pattern of habit. He talked aloud to himself in his perplexity and despair: "Go to Bethlehem . . . How can I take Mary to Bethlehem? . . . She can't walk that distance . . . and the sway of donkey travel would be as upsetting as walking! We're not going . . ."

✦ ✦ ✦

Joseph had never imagined that life could be so disturbing as it had been in these recent months. First, there had been those doubts about Mary . . . and the child. And although he hadn't really understood, he had been reassured, and in his love for her he accepted it all for fact, trusting that somehow the Lord God would make clear to him how and why Mary was to be God's chosen instrument for being mother to Israel's Savior. It had been almost more than a man's mind could stand. And now this unexpected turn of Caesar's whim . . . And Mary near the end of her time—How could she possibly stand the journey. The Caesars—What right had they to . . . ?

The donkeys by their own leading turned in at the path that brought them home. They were almost at the stable door before Joseph realized where he was. Without stopping to unload the beasts, he hurried into the house. "Mary," he burst out, "how can you possibly make that journey? You aren't strong enough! It isn't fair to you . . . or to him. The Caesars are the curse of the world. Would to God that someone would arise who would free us and all mankind from them!"

Mary broke in. "The Lord God will do that in his own good time, Joseph. But what do you mean? You say that I can't go on a journey. I hadn't planned to go on any journey, Joseph. How could I, even if I wanted to . . . with him . . . coming so soon?"

"Well, you have to go on a journey. Caesar Augustus says so."

"Me, Joseph? Why me?" Mary asked quietly.

"Oh, I don't mean just you. All of us—all our people—have to go, each to our native city, to register before the end of December. It's for a tax. Naaman told me about it. He was terribly angry." Joseph half smiled as he remembered Naaman's outburst. Then his face hardened. "You can't go. It's impossible."

Mary's answer had the wisdom of inevitability, a wisdom that some women and fewer men have: "Joseph, if we have to go, we will go."

✦ ✦ ✦

The days that followed were uneasy for Mary and Joseph. How much would the trip cost? How much would they have left in their reserve? (If they had ever imagined that their journey would also take them to Egypt, they would have despaired. But that part of the journey was God's doing.) How would they travel? When would they leave?

Day after day they delayed. It was now the latter part of the month. They could delay no longer, for before that week's end, they had to be in Bethlehem. Next midmorning they set out—for "Bethlehem of Judea."

✦ ✦ ✦

And what of the Caesars? The Caesars never care about what happens to people uprooted because of their orders. Human lives are simply currency with which they buy what they want. The fact that one woman great with child or a thousand women carrying unborn children were traveling roads and highways, enduring the discomforts and perils of a forced journey, meant nothing to them. And the Caesars would never have understood that a child to be born of a woman traveling to Bethlehem would be the power that eventually would tear their empire apart.

✦ ✦ ✦

72

It seemed to Joseph that they would never come within sight of Bethlehem—they had had to travel so slowly! For all Mary's courage, there were many times when they had had to stop and rest—much against her will. Often Joseph's hand had reached out to rest against Mary's weary body to give her support. And often he had moistened her dry lips and wiped the dust from her face.

Suddenly Joseph turned in apprehension, for he heard the rhythmic tread of a marching Roman legion and the clank of their light armor. They were coming along the same highway on which he and Mary were traveling. Joseph saw that before him and behind him pilgrims like themselves were scurrying off the highway like rabbits at the sound of the hunter's approach.

Joseph, realizing Mary's exhaustion, knew that they could not possibly flee into the fields to find protection from the legion's arrogance. He led the donkey that carried Mary to the edge of the road, and the forlorn couple kept their plodding way. But for Joseph and Mary to have stepped aside was not deference enough to suit the Roman officer. As he passed, he struck Joseph's donkey a heavy blow with the flat of his sword. The stolid beast, bearing the precious burden of Mary (who herself carried the infinitely precious burden of the Son of God), reared and galloped off the road, down the bank, and half fell into the ditch below. Horror-stricken, Joseph leaped headlong after the frightened beast. In an effort that had the strength of love and fear, and something of his hatred of the Caesars, within it, he grasped at the loose bridle, while with the other hand he sustained the falling woman, great with child. A roar of hard laughter from the ranks of the soldiery followed him as they saw the near-tragic episode. The captain smiled grimly.

"See the Jew," shouted one of the rear rank soldiers. "Who is more afraid, he or his donkey?"

"Hard to tell," called another. "They're both related." And that sally of humor brought more laughter.

As the soldiers marched by, their feet raised clouds of dust that were blown across the fields, and the dust settled over Mary and Joseph like light brown pigment. It filled their eyes and nostrils and caked their parched lips.

Joseph wiped Mary's face as best he could. Tenderly, he touched her eyes. He moistened her lips with a damp cloth and then opened their water bottle. In it there was left a single mouthful of water. It was warm, fouled by the dust, but Mary swallowed gratefully. Resting on the support of Joseph's arm, she whispered, "Joseph—how can I go on?"

"It isn't far, Mary," Joseph urged. "Come!"

In his determination that they should be on their way to safety and shelter, Joseph did what he had never done before. He struck the donkey with a tree branch that had been lying in the ditch beside them, and pushing and hauling and urging the frightened animal, he almost carried it up the embankment to the solid surface of the highway.

And their faces were once again set toward Bethlehem.

As Mary and Joseph went on, the travail of a woman in labor came upon Mary. Hands clenched, breathing deeply and with effort, Mary tried to close the door of consciousness on weariness and pain. Finally they were in the front courtyard of the Bethlehem Inn.

But, as the New Testament says, "there was no room for them in the inn."

✦ ✦ ✦

Many have said that it was not the fault of anyone in Bethlehem that that night there was no room for Mary and Joseph in the inn—yet, somehow, it was the fault of everyone. Of course, the servants at the inn were busy, overworked, meeting the demands of the patrons of the overcrowded hostel. Yet surely, someone among them all might have recognized human need. But individual need rarely moves us as it should. We have eyes, and we see, but we do not understand. They too had eyes, but they did not understand.

And, the realists ask: "Why exchange a night's sleep for fulfilling an impulse to help two dust-covered travelers? Anyway, they should have been at the inn earlier in the day—like the rest of us room-renters!" And, having eyes, the realists do not understand.

✦ ✦ ✦

But there was Simon the innkeeper—Simon who alone did something to give shelter to Mary and Joseph. Did he not turn his favorite horse out to stand in the cold night wind, so that Mary could have that fresh, clean stall in the stable? Without Simon's help and sympathy, the very plans of God might have gone awry.

After Mary had come into the warmth and shelter of the stable, it was evident that before another hour had passed, the child would be born.

Meanwhile Mary had no answers for the questions which in her moments of freedom from pain she had been asking herself: If she were fulfilling God's purpose, why this nightmarish journey? And why had she had to come to this—to a stable for his birthplace? She doubted the very word of the Lord spoken to her by the angel. She wondered—Could not the Lord God do better than this for her son—his Son—even in spite of the Caesars and the crowds?

✦ ✦ ✦

Simon went to the inn kitchen after having shown the weary couple to their temporary shelter. There he saw Susanna, a serving maid, exchanging banter with the cook. With a word of rebuke, he ordered her to the stable to give Mary such help as she needed.

Susanna had stood beside many a woman in that lonely hour of human birth. But she had never seen it like this. There was an inner strength in this woman—this . . . "Mary," as she remembered hearing Joseph call her. It was a strength that came from—God knew where. She made no outcry. It was almost as if she took joy in the final time of her travail, knowing that what she endured was little compared to giving life to him whom she was bearing. This lack of outcry, this absence of cursing and railing which Susanna had usually heard in such hours, this sense of assured strength in the frail body, this seeming surety that the child was worth it all—these things perplexed Susanna, but only briefly—for constantly, even as her hands were busy, her mind was skipping hither and yon, occupied with her own affairs. Susanna's fitful moments of kindness were never dominant, for she was the captive of her own desires.

When finally the child lay beside his mother, Susanna, looking first at him, and then at Mary and Joseph, exclaimed: "He's like neither of you. He's a different breed. I never saw one like him. People of many races and lands stop here at the inn, but he is kin to none of them, either . . ." And then her voice took on a pitch of excitement. "And yet—he reminds me of them all!"

Susanna turned to go. "I've got to leave—I have things to do. You're all right now," she said to Mary. Mary nodded her thanks, for words were still physically far beyond her. She reached out her hand toward Susanna as if to hold the presence of another woman with her for just a little longer. But Susanna was on her way, concerned only with her own affairs.

In the early-morning hours Susanna turned down the path toward the little dwelling where her family lived. Her sister was awake. Susanna yawned. "What a day! There are too many people in the world, and most of them are at the Bethlehem Inn. I'll tell you about it in the morning." And she was asleep.

Susanna had not noticed the star. She never heard the angels sing, for she had not remained with Mary. In Susanna's eyes, Mary and the child really meant nothing out of the ordinary, even though the extraordinary was around them both.

But because of that night's experience, Susanna did not marry the Bethlehem carpenter, Joab, who wanted her for his wife. She said: "Carpenters aren't able to provide for their families. That carpenter—What was his name? Joseph? He couldn't do better than a stable for his wife. Not for me! I'll marry Ezra the merchant from north of Jerusalem. I'll let Joab go, and take Ezra's comfort any day." She did not understand the joy and peace of true affection such as Mary and Joseph knew—affection that binds two people together for time and eternity.

Having eyes, Susanna did not see.

✦ ✦ ✦

There was another who saw the events of that night. He was a watcher through the gap in a broken board—Ezra, the stableboy.

Ezra was upset when Simon turned his favorite horse out into the courtyard cold for the sake of two strangers. Ezra covered the horse with a blanket; he laid his face against the horse's neck, and patting him in affection, he said: "I never thought Simon would treat you like this. They aren't worth it. Simon's become an easy mark."

"Ezra!" The boy jumped, startled. It was Simon. "Go and feed the cattle."

"Yes, sir." Ezra was angry. He was above that kind of work; he was a stableboy for horses, not for cows. That lout Esau, who had disappeared that afternoon—this was his job. But Ezra knew better than to question Simon's orders.

Slowly Ezra went through the courtyard to the rear of the stables, where the cattle were. The last stall backed up against the place where Simon's horse was kept. As Ezra fed the cattle, he worked his way to the end shelter. He seemed to hear voices. The sound came through from the front wall of the end stall. Pushing his way through the darkness, he noticed a broken board. Lifting it aside, he heard and saw what was forever to be the most vivid memory of his life.

As Ezra looked in open-eyed wonder, he saw kings, walking directly toward the horse stall. And there in the stall were the man and the woman. And there was a baby lying in the manger. That's what the woman was watching—a baby! For a moment Ezra forgot about the kings. So that's what all the commotion was about in the kitchen when they tried to tell him they weren't talking about anything in particular—they knew what was going on—

they thought he wouldn't understand.

But now he knew something they didn't know. Kings! If they knew that, they'd all be running outside as fast as they could to see! Kings!—and in Simon's stable!

The kings came near the manger. They knelt. They placed handwrought leather boxes on the straw-covered floor before the child. After making their obeisance, they withdrew. And in the silence that followed, Ezra thought that he could hear the shuffle of camels walking. But he was too excited, too bewildered, to leave his spy-hole to find out.

If only he had gold like that in those boxes, then he and David could go away together, as they wanted to do in the plans they shared with each other.

Why had these kings come to Simon's stable. Why did they treat that woman like . . . like a queen . . . and treat the baby as if he himself were a king over them? . . . and why? . . . and why? . . . and Ezra fell asleep.

In the morning the hot breath of a nuzzling cow hungry for breakfast wakened Ezra. Stiff and cramped, he wondered how he could have fallen asleep. Then the remembrance of what he had seen brought him to his feet in excitement. Away he ran, without thought of anything else, to tell them at home what he had seen.

"Father, he was a lovely baby . . . He was more than a baby . . . I don't know just what . . . And, Father, you should have seen those kings! You never saw so many jewels in your life, some of them big as pigeon eggs!"

Ezra's mother was uneasy and pained. Why did Ezra exaggerate? How could he possibly make all this up . . . and expect them to believe it? But Ezra's father quieted her attempts to stop the boy and upbraid him, and he bade Ezra continue.

"Father, if I had money like that, Bethlehem couldn't hold me. Nothing ever happens here. Maybe I should have tried to get taken on as servant to one of those kings. Bet I could look after camels!"

But it would not have been the King of Kings to whom Ezra would have given himself in service that day, for, like many of us, he was dazzled by the gold and the precious stones. Having eyes, the lad saw not—certainly not as he later came to see.

✦ ✦ ✦

Generation after generation, the child born that night moves as a man among us in our world, and so often he goes unrecognized. He is always beside us, and we are especially aware of his presence on Christmas Eve. May it not be said of us: "And having eyes, they do not see, and they understand not."

TELL ME HIS NAME

TELL ME HIS NAME

T HE GOSPEL of Matthew says: "And being warned of God in a dream that they should not return to Herod, the wise men departed into their own country another way."

Their camels were led out of the stable yard, the baggage loaded, the riders seated, and then that shuffling noise which camels' feet always make gradually died away in the distance. The last of the unexpected night visitors had left the stable. And the little family—three in number now—was alone. The bright light from the sky, which had for a time illumined the stable with the brightness of day, had disappeared. Only a lantern's modest, warm glow shone over the mother, and over the child, who was lying in the woman's arms. In the half-dark, outside the little circle of lantern light, was the man, resting upon piled straw.

✦ ✦ ✦

After the excitement and wonder of the past hours, it was strangely quiet and peaceful in that hour of predawn when day still sleeps and night has not yet left on its noiseless wings. In that quiet and peace the breathing of the animals seemed loud—and yet far away.

The child was asleep. For a time no word was spoken. Mary and Joseph were still turmoiled by all that had happened. As Mary remembered in detail the events of the night, the glory of wonder shone in her eyes—the glory that is in the eyes of any woman who has borne a son to whom honor has come. Mary, even though she had been blessed of God, was a woman, with a woman's heart, and she desired for her son recognition and honor.

Joseph was remembering too. He was remembering how in the late afternoon he had been in the depths of a man's despair. He who had promised to provide for Mary as long as life lasted could provide no place for the fulfillment of her life—the birth of the child. Neither his persuasion nor his slender moneybag was able to open any door for him and his wife. Finally they had found their refuge—in a stable, along with the beasts of the field. For him, that was the hour of his deepest humiliation. Fear and bitterness had been in his heart—fear for Mary and for their child; and as he watched her travail, there was bitterness, bitterness toward Rome, indeed bitterness toward all mankind.

Although Joseph was not the first man hurt through adversity that came to his family, it seemed to him that no man had ever suffered as he had. But now the bitterness had disappeared, the fear had vanished; and as he sat outside the circle of light watching mother and son, he remembered other things that had happened that night, and he knew both exultation and uneasy wonder.

✦ ✦ ✦

Mary moved carefully to ease her position so as not to disturb the child, and as she did, her movement drew Joseph back to reality.

"Mary, are you all right? Will you . . . can you . . . rest?"

"I'm resting, Joseph."

"No, Mary, I mean . . . can you sleep?"

She shook her head.

"Mary, I do not understand. Why are you not exhausted? When you reached here after the journey, you could not even stand by yourself . . . and you have borne a child . . . and this has been a night of happenings such as we would not have dared even imagine."

"O Joseph, do you not understand? My weariness is forgotten in the wonder of it. I need no rest . . . if I only remember."

And then, as if he could not believe what had come, Joseph said, almost in disbelief, "It all happened, didn't it, Mary?"

"Certainly it happened, Joseph," said Mary. "See, beside the manger—the leathern wrought boxes with the gold, the frankincense, the myrrh."

Joseph reached over and opened the box left by Numbidian. He closed his hand among the gold coins, to let them fall, clinking, through his fingers.

"And see, Joseph," Mary added, "there beside you are the shepherds' gifts."

✦ ✦ ✦

Mary asked Joseph to lay the child in his manger bed. And carefully, with that tumult in his breast which all men know when they hold their firstborn in their arms, he placed the child in the manger, where, a brief hour before, as an unheeding babe he had been holding court for the wise men from afar.

The wondering, pent-up excitement of Joseph and Mary could be restrained no longer, and their tongues were unloosed. As the one stopped, the other took it up. They went over and over the events of that wondrous night, as if two were telling a single tale.

"Joseph, what would we have done without the serving girl from the inn? . . . I was afraid of her when she first came in—her hard voice and her coarse words. And then . . . it all seemed to disappear as she helped me and cared for me when I needed her most. Did you see the stableboy?" And Mary laughed as she thought of the lad.

"What stableboy, Mary?"

"Why, Joseph, how could you have missed him? How could you have missed his big wondering eyes, even if you missed the boy himself? But the girl sent him flying."

"Mary, there was the light. I have never seen it so bright. And there was the music such as I have never heard. I thought my mind was fevered. But the others heard it too."

"Joseph—the shepherds . . . How did they know?"

"Why, Mary, they said that the angel of the Lord told them. And they said that out yonder on the hills they heard the music that we heard . . . But the wise men, Mary—How did they know?"

"Don't you remember? They said that it was in their books that when the star shone near and white, it foretold that the expected child would be born in Bethlehem of Judea in a manger. And the promise was that the star would lead those who followed it to him. Joseph, it is as I was told before he came . . . that he was to be . . .

more than just a son born to you and me."

"Yes, Mary, our son is high among the sons of David."

"No, Joseph, it is more than that. He is Son of God . . . of the household of God. That is more than David and his sons, and more than all Israel."

Joseph could hardly believe that he had heard Mary aright.

"Mary," he said, "you are tired. You do not know what it is that you say. Why, to belong to the house of David is the highest place our nation knows."

"Not nearly as high, Joseph, as to belong to the household of God."

And as he had done so many times lately, Joseph looked in wonder at Mary. Constantly she surprised him, because so often she seemed to be much more than the peasant girl whom he had known. Her mind seemed to range until it came into the very presence of the Lord God himself.

And then they talked of the child, of their new life as a family; of what he would be; of what they must do. And Mary vowed that no day would pass without her prayers to God for him.

✦ ✦ ✦

The light of dawn came as they were talking, and in the little shed next to the stable a rooster was crowing in the day with the braggadocio of one who feels that he is responsible for its promise.

Dawn meant that the servants of the inn were up and about. Excited, they heard the news that in the stable a child had been born during the night. The cook and his helper, the maids and the porter—and the stableboy with them—hurried across the yard to peer in upon the little family. There in the shadows (for the light of the lantern had gone out) they could see the child resting in the manger, the woman lying on the straw fast asleep, and the man standing, watching.

As they began to talk outside the door in excited whispers, Joseph turned and placed his finger on his lips to quiet them. He moved toward the door to answer their questions. But the stableboy forestalled Joseph, for he was saying: "I watched it all last night . . . I would have seen more, but Susanna put me out when the woman cried . . . and I saw the shepherds come, and then the kings with their camels and servants and gold and jewels. They stayed and only left just before dawn. I stood behind the manger. See that loose board—I moved it over and I was able to see." And then his perplexed voice asked, "Why should they have come to see this child and this family, and them not able to get a room in our inn?"

Of a sudden they all turned upon the boy to tell him it could not be true, that he had too much imagination—to tell him that when his mother heard that he had no truth in his bones, she would know how to deal with him.

They were ready to scold him further when across the courtyard came the serving girl who had helped Mary in her hour of need. They gathered around her, for she had much to tell. "I was with her," she said, "when the child was born. There is more in this than just the birth of a child to that carpenter and his wife. The glory of the Lord shone round about them. And I heard music such as I have never heard, and there was a light that no lantern could ever bring. And as I was leaving, the shepherds came, shepherds who said that they had been sent by the angel of the Lord. And I doubt it not."

They wondered, for this was the woman whom they

had known to be sharp of tongue, with ways of life that left much to be desired. It was as if she were a new woman, as if she had been reborn that night. They listened in silence, then went back to the inn subdued by what they had seen and heard.

✦ ✦ ✦

The day passed quietly enough. Joseph was kept busy meeting the needs of his family, seeing that there was food for Mary and that she was comfortable.

Mary dozed and wakened, and wakening she remembered—as she remembered each day for the rest of her life. And then she was asleep again. And so the day passed.

✦ ✦ ✦

That night after Joseph had bedded himself in the straw, he dreamed a dream in which he was directed by the Almighty to flee in haste with the child and his mother to Egypt. The dream was so vivid that on waking he could not rid himself of the belief that the voice of God had actually spoken to him. He was profoundly disturbed, and the more so as he remembered the wise men's concern. They too had been warned in a dream, and the dream had to do with the child. The wise men were told to avoid Jerusalem because of danger that would come to the child if they were to return there. Certainly he and Mary ought not to be any less careful than the wise men had been.

When Mary wakened from her long night's sleep, Joseph's first words to her were: "Mary, this night we must leave. We have been warned of God in a dream that we must go to Egypt."

Mary sighed, for her weary body, asserting itself, had almost overpowered her spirit. "O Joseph, how can I?"

"But, Mary, we must go—it is for the child."

And that decided it.

"All right, Joseph. And it is to be tonight?"

"Tonight, Mary."

✦ ✦ ✦

Then suddenly Joseph exclaimed, "Why, Mary, I must register the child, the child and ourselves!"

"O Joseph—not the child!"

"Yes, he must be registered now . . . of the house and lineage of David. That is what those Romans demand of us—every man and woman and child registered, so that the tax burden can be increased."

"But, Joseph, I cannot take him."

"I shall take him, Mary. It is only across the courtyard and into the inn, where they have set up their office. And I shall take him now."

Mary, who had first taken up the child as if to protect him, gave him into Joseph's arms with loving care. It was his first journey into the world—and away from her. Mary's arms seemed empty—as her arms seemed empty when she stood beneath the cross thirty-three years later —and in that hour she remembered this first loneliness of separation from her Son.

It was the final day for registering. It seemed as if all the people had already registered, for the Roman authorities were preparing to leave, their census work finished. Joseph appeared at the booth just inside the front door of the inn. The Roman officer Marius and his helper Lucius were already packing the records, those endless records which governments from time immemorial have kept. Joseph waited, as befitted the citizen of a subject people, but there was no response. Finally he broke the silence to say, "I have come to register."

"You're late. Why weren't you here yesterday?"

"I couldn't come yesterday."

"It's like you Jews to leave it till the last minute. Lucius, where is that last tablet?"

"Marius, it is full."

"Well, we've got to get this man's name on it and the child's name. And I suppose the child has a mother?" he added brutally.

"Yes, I want to register for myself, my wife, and our child."

"Where is the woman?"

"Well, the boy is only a day and a half old, and she couldn't come."

"All right. What are the names?"

"I am Joseph and she is Mary . . . and he . . . well, we shall name him, when the time comes, Jesus."

"Ah, you Jews! You won't let it die, will you? Jesus! That is the name of one of your heroes! And so you think he will be a hero too, and perhaps drive us Romans out Palestine . . . But don't let him try. Lucius, how do you think he would look with a sword in his hand and a helmet and a breastplate, facing the Roman legions?" The man laughed, and then he said, almost to himself, "These cursed people—you can't break their spirit!"

As he spoke, at the very end of the tablet he was writing the names, and the very last name he wrote was "Jesus"—"of the house and lineage of David." As he struggled to get the letters into the little space that remained, he repeated what he was writing, naming the child and his ancestry. As he spoke, Joseph was recalling aloud to himself what Mary had said: ". . . of the house and the lineage of God." The officer, half hearing him, and not catching the last words, broke in, "Make up your mind, man—Is it of the house of David or not?"

Joseph nodded and held the child more closely.

"Well, don't stand there. On your way—that's all."

✦ ✦ ✦

Lucius was barely twenty. He was new to the Roman legions and their ways. He watched, and as he heard Marius talk to Joseph, he was moved as he had not been during all that week in which he had seen hundreds and hundreds of people. He was uneasy about this man Joseph because of his bearing and because of the way he held the child and watched over him—as if he were the kin of an emperor. Joseph seemed to know something about the child that he had not told. Certainly it was not all summed up in the name "Jesus" and "of the house and lineage of David." What could it be?

Lucius held the door as Joseph passed through. As Joseph went by him, Lucius said: "Marius doesn't really mean it. He is busy and hard, it's his way of talking." The door closed, and Joseph and Lucius were outside.

Lucius said: "That is a fine boy you have. He will make a good man." Then, fearing that he had said too much, he turned hastily and went back into the inn.

That night Joseph and Mary and the child were on their way to Egypt.

✦ ✦ ✦

The next day, while waiting for the horses for the Roman captain and himself, Lucius heard from Susanna the story of the birth of the child. When the young Roman had first come to Bethlehem, he and Susanna had exchanged many flippant, bandying words. But now it was a different Susanna, subdued, changed, for she could not forsake the conviction that she had witnessed something far greater than she understood.

✦ ✦ ✦

Eventually Lucius went to Britain to help build and garrison the Roman forts in that outpost of the empire. In his service of the Roman emperor he marched as soldier and officer over much of Europe. And during the years of his service Lucius became a highly skilled professional soldier.

There came a day when Lucius was sent to the territory around Capernaum with the rank of centurion. There he was respected and regarded with as deep affection as an occupied people ever give to the representatives of their foreign rulers. Lucius understood and respected the Hebrew people. There in Capernaum he helped the native people build a new and more adequate synagogue so that they might the more properly worship Jehovah, the God of their fathers.

Lucius began to hear much about an extraordinary traveling rabbi, a man who had power even to heal the sick. He was interested to see and to hear this teacher. And now the word was that the rabbi was coming directly to Capernaum. Lucius was glad, for the sake of his own curiosity, and for the sake of his beloved personal servant who was ill. This man had served Lucius faithfully and well for many years, but now he was sick nigh unto death and the medical skill of the day could avail him nothing.

In desperation Lucius besought the elders of the synagogue in Capernaum to appeal to this traveling rabbi to see if he would bring his healing powers to bear on his servant friend. The elders made their plea, and Jesus listened with interest.

Word spread through the community that Jesus was on his way to the centurion's house. Lucius sent friends to say that such a personal visit was not necessary, for all that the rabbi needed to do was to speak the word and the servant would be healed. Lucius, through his friends, further explained that he himself knew what it was to exercise authority, and certainly the rabbi had authority sufficient to bring about the healing even though he himself did not appear. Jesus, marveling at the centurion's faith, said, "I have not found so great faith, no, not in Israel."

That evening Lucius went to the home where Jesus was being given hospitality, in order to thank Jesus personally for what he had done for his servant. As they talked together, it was clear to Lucius that here was one who differed from any other religious teacher whom he had ever met. And then, in one of those strange flashes of realization that come to men when the mind suddenly recalls a forgotten fact, Lucius said excitedly, incredulously: "Your name is Jesus! Yes, now I know. You were born in Bethlehem of Judea, weren't you?"

Jesus answered, "Yes."

Lucius continued, his voice unsteady because of his wondering excitement: "I was there when your father registered you with the Roman captain Marius. Your mother . . . she could not come, for you had just been born. And to think that I should see you again, with

God's hand upon you as you minister to your people."

Jesus, looking on him, loved him, and replied, "Not only to my people, Lucius, but to all people, for there is neither Jew nor Gentile, we are all sons of him who is my Father."

And that night Christ was born again—born in the heart of Lucius, not as a child, but as the Son of God, the Lord of Lucius' life.

HE GAVE MORE
THAN HE KNEW

HE GAVE MORE
THAN HE KNEW

I N THE FALL of the year three kings, Numbidian, Kelsorius, and Telfima, met in Ecbatana. They met to talk of political alliances, but they and their astrologers and wise men had another concern. They were concerned because of the discovery of a new star, different from any other they knew. Their astrologers and priests had come across a prophecy in Babylon, written at the time of the Jewish exile. It told that a star in the east would foretell the birth of one who would be the universal ruler, and that, as it moved across the heavens, it would lead the traveler to the very place where the ruler would be born.

As the kings discussed the prophecy, inevitably they began to wonder if a political alliance might not be expedient, for if an alliance were made with the counselors of this universal ruler at the beginning of his life, they would be among those who had first paid him homage.

Political expediency, curiosity, and a sense of reverence led the three kings to decide to make the journey from the east, following the star. They felt that their final destination would prove to be Jerusalem, for only in the capital city would such a momentous birth take place.

There is no adequate record of this journey which finally brought Numbidian, Kelsorius, and Telfima to the birthplace of the Christ-child. We depend upon a few sentences in Matthew's Gospel, our knowledge of the life of that day, a few words of historical tradition, and upon reverent Christian imagination. And so we make the journey with them.

✦ ✦ ✦

Numbidian, Kelsorius, Telfima, journeying farther and farther into alien lands, repeatedly asked themselves if theirs was a fool's enterprise. Daytime travel was filled with uncertainty. But when night fell, certainty always returned, for there in the heavens was the star. It grew in brightness and magnitude with the passing hours.

The three kings reached Palestine. Travel was now more difficult. The highways were filled with men and women and children, a crisscrossing tide of humanity ebbing and flowing across the countryside, each family seeking its town of origin, there to register in the census ordered by Caesar Augustus.

✦ ✦ ✦

The three kings came to Jerusalem. As rulers from foreign lands, they paid their courtesy respects to Herod. His curiosity and suspicion were ill-concealed. In answer to his direct questioning, they told him why they had come to Jerusalem and of him whom they hoped to find. Herod was both pleased and fearful. Who could this interloper be who drew foreign rulers from the ends of the earth?

His insistence was mingled with apprehension and anger, as he urged the three kings, after their search, to return to share his hospitality and tell him where the child was, that he too might go and bring him gifts.

✦ ✦ ✦

The kings and their company encamped near a pool of water two miles outside the walls of Jerusalem. They sat long in Numbidian's tent, profoundly disturbed by Herod's implacable hostility toward their errand. As darkness settled over the city and the encampment, the kings called their astrologers to take the celestial observations, that the kings might be reassured as on each previous night since the journey began.

But never had the star shone as now! There, over the nearby hill town of Bethlehem, was the star that had been their constant companion. Never had it shone with such brilliance. As they watched, they realized that the star stood still. Was this the night for which they had been waiting? Was the little town of Bethlehem, rather than Jerusalem, the place of the foretold event toward which they had been traveling these many weeks? Had he really come, as the old records said he would? With common consent they agreed that they would go to Bethlehem, that they might see if it had come to pass.

✦ ✦ ✦

They drew near the town, and there, lower than they had ever seen it, the star that had led them seemed to be hanging, pendant-like, from the skies. Incredulously they saw that it was immediately over a stable behind the inn.

101

How could it be that he whom they had sought, whose coming was foretold by portents in the heavens, was housed among the cattle? They stopped, doubting and irresolute, before the doorway.

When courage and faith had grown low in the past, Numbidian had ever been the man of hope and of deeds. So it was now. Pointing to the stable, he said: "What better place for the birth of a great one? Who would look for him here? Born in this place, he may well forestall the suspicion and vengeance of Herod. Look around you! Saw you ever such a night? The star is here, and there is the place. We go in!"

They dismounted. The bearers accompanied them to the stable door. Numbidian, Kelsorius, and Telfima, each took from the bearers his box of treasure. The door was partly ajar, and through the opening they saw the divine-human drama of the Holy Family, the scene that has baffled and perplexed more people than any other scene in history. There was Mary, upon whom the hand of God had been placed; the child was sleeping the sleep of all newborn life; and the man, Joseph, was standing by, puzzled and abashed by the bewildering strangeness of the events of the night.

As the kings entered, they saw, bending in adoration, shepherds and a lad. In a moment the shepherds and the lad arose to go. As they departed, the door swung wide, and the kings heard singing voices, richer and fuller than any they had ever known. And each man recognized the words as if sung in his own tongue: "Glory to God in the highest, and on earth peace, good will toward men."

This strange scene, this humble place, were not what the kings had expected. But an angelic choir was better authentication than a panoplied guard of court attendants.

The light of the star and the radiance of the presence of God in the midst of the simplicity of the humble surroundings were more powerfully compelling than a salute of trumpets. With no word one to the other, each knelt and placed before the child and the mother his treasure— gold, frankincense, and myrrh.

Numbidian, who alone spoke the Hebrew tongue, addressed Joseph. "We have come from afar. We have been led by the star in the heavens. For weeks we have hoped against hope that we would find him who was to be born this night, the universal king. And it is even as the ancient teachers have said. Our devotion and our allegiance are his."

+ + +

Sleep was long in coming to the kings in those early-morning hours. The glory of the Lord was other than they had expected, and they talked wonderingly. When sleep did come, it was troubled. Near dawn Numbidian dreamed a dream that had the clarity of events in real life. In it he was told that he and his fellow kings must depart immediately and get as far from the city of Jerusalem as they could! So real was the dream that after the morning meal Numbidian went by himself back to Bethlehem. There in the courtyard he met Joseph. "Joseph," he said, "last night after I had seen the mother and the child, in my sleep it was as if the voice of the gods spoke to me to say: 'Go not back to Jerusalem to tell Herod of what you have seen. Return by another way.' Joseph, you and the child and Mary are in great danger. Have a care!"

+ + +

When the same morrow dawned for the Holy Family, the events of the night had been so extraordinary as to make them doubt that they had really happened. And yet how could they doubt! There before them were hand-wrought boxes such as no Hebrew had ever made, containing gold and frankincense and myrrh.

That same day, Simon the innkeeper was able to find room for the Holy Family in the inn because of a departing guest. The next day, Joseph, waking in the early-morning hours, was deeply troubled. He had dreamed that the angel of the Lord had said: "Arise, and take the young child and his mother, and flee into Egypt, and be thou there until I bring thee word: for Herod will seek the young child to destroy him."

✦ ✦ ✦

Late that afternoon information came to Herod that the three kings had been seen departing from his country. They had disobeyed his instructions! They had not come back to Jerusalem! Fear, suspicion, a sense of being duped, joined to make his immediate action prompt, decisive, vicious. "They have found him whom they sought," he said, "and they have kept from me where he is." His orders were ruthless: "Kill all children under two years of age." Thus and thus alone could he be sure that the child whom the kings from the east had found would never come to a place of power.

The cruel order shocked even the hardened consciences of his mercenaries. And for long sorrow-stricken months, the cry of Rachel for her children was heard throughout the land.

✦ ✦ ✦

That night when darkness fell, Mary and Joseph and the child left the inn, that they might make their way to Egypt even as the angel of the Lord had directed them.

At this point there is a gap in the Scripture record. It gives no explanation of how Joseph could take Mary and the newborn child to a foreign land, and there live for long months, and then come back to Palestine to pick up work and life in Nazareth. The way in which all this became possible depended on Numbidian and his gift.

✦ ✦ ✦

When in the morning hours, before their departure from Bethlehem, Joseph had told Mary of his dream and had expressed his concern and fear, Mary showed no surprise. For to Mary there had come, with a certainty that Joseph did not as yet know, the realization that God was using the little family for his own purpose.

Joseph was apprehensive. He had always done for Mary, and he would always do for Mary and his child as a man of his means and resources was able. But a journey to Egypt was beyond anything he could possibly attempt. "If we go to Egypt," he asked, "how shall we live? Why, we have brought scarce enough money to last us one more week here at the inn!"

Came Mary's answer: "The way will be provided, Joseph." And imperceptibly her hand reached out to touch the handwrought box that Numbidian had left.

✦ ✦ ✦

The family traveled whenever possible by night. By day they sought the back lanes and rough roads. They rested in as isolated areas as they could without arousing suspicion. There came an afternoon when they expected to leave Herod's territory. Yonder were the boundary markers. No one was in sight. Soon there would be safety, and freedom from fear and from the hand of Herod. But hope died even in the moment that it rose high, for a soldier stood across the way.

Peremptorily the soldier called out, "Where to?"

"My wife and I are on a journey," replied Joseph.

"Your wife? Let me see . . . Ah, yes, your wife—and that is your child too! And so you thought to escape Herod's orders! You Hebrews are always trying to evade the law. But this time you shall not." He reached to take the child from the arms of the mother.

Mary, body taut, face white, raised a hand to interpose. And as she did, of a sudden she asked, "Have you children of your own?" Startled, the soldier nodded. "Then," said Mary, "you know what it is to hold a child in your arms even as I hold my child." Before any word could be said in reply, she had opened Numbidian's box, and taking two of the heavy gold coins, she laid them in the soldier's palm.

He looked in amazement. How could peasants like these have such coins?—and of such weight? Why, they were worth more than he received from the emperor's paymaster for a year's service as a soldier! But he was more than amazed. He was disconcerted. Never had man's mind and heart been searched as his had been searched by the eyes of the woman while she pleaded for her child. He stood in indecisiveness as the little family moved on. In a moment they had crossed the dividing line into the adjoining country. Almost unaware that they had gone, he watched them go, while he was saying to him-

106

self: "If it were my child . . . If it were my child . . ."

And Numbidian had given more than he knew.

✦ ✦ ✦

As they put the safety of distance between themselves and the soldier, Joseph's eyes were uneasy. They glanced first at Mary, then at the child, then at the far horizon. It was as if he had been further unsettled by another bewildering discovery. Never had he suspected that such resoluteness lived within Mary's gentle beauty. It was as if he were upbraiding himself for failing to act as he asked, "Mary, what led you to do that?"

"Joseph," she answered, "what else was there to do? Numbidian brought the gold for our child. What better way to use it than to save his life? Surely the king would have approved of that."

✦ ✦ ✦

The journey was now easier. The hand of fear was no longer driving them on. Toward the latter part of February they reached the city of Raamses, and there they settled. Egypt, the land of bondage from which their Hebrew forefathers had been freed by Moses, was now the unwitting haven of safety for one greater than Moses, one for whom the whole Hebrew nation had yearned and hoped over many centuries.

✦ ✦ ✦

In the city of Raamses they lived simply on a side street, and so unobtrusively that none wondered greatly about the foreign couple and their child. The woman, as

107

she walked abroad, met all inquiring glances with a friendliness that defeated prying curiosity and forestalled hostility. The neighbors showed her the acts of kindness and affection that mark neighbors all over the world.

But it was of the child that the women spoke most frequently. The child seemed to have the wisdom of all time in his eyes as he watched men and women, the passing light and shadow, and the animals of the neighborhood.

One pattern of the family's life, however, was a matter for conjecture. Occasionally Joseph went away for long days on end, and no one knew where. And always the mother and child waited uneasily for his return.

The odd jobs that came a carpenter's way never provided enough to maintain the little family in food and clothes and shelter. Therefore, from time to time Joseph journeyed to Alexandria, the most cosmopolitan city in Egypt, to seek out the money changers who dealt in the currencies of the world. There he exchanged the gold coins from Numbidian's kingdom for the currency of Egypt. Always one coin and no more. Always it was Mary who decided that the time had come when Joseph should journey to Alexandria.

Joseph received far less in drachmas than Numbidian's coin was worth. But Joseph never argued, for a peasant with a heavy gold coin could so easily be killed in a strange city by gold-hungry men, and no word would be said. What he received in exchange was small matter, as long as food could be bought and life lived.

✦ ✦ ✦

The child was nearly two years old. Once again the Word of God came to Joseph in a dream: "Arise, and take

the young child and his mother, and go into the land of
Israel: for they are dead which sought the young child's
life." Mary and Joseph saw no reason to doubt. They had
lived by the Word of God as it had come to them before,
and by the direction of that Word they would continue to
act.

After unexplained "good-bys," they set out to return to
their native land. And Numidian's gold finally brought
them back to Nazareth, this town which was to be forever
remembered because the days of their son's childhood
were lived there.

Numbidian had given more than he knew.

✦ ✦ ✦

Over the years in the life of a busy household, the night
of wonder years ago in Bethlehem and the months spent
in Egypt began to seem like a tale told to someone else, a
tale which Mary and Joseph were simply recalling in
memory. But there were times when, after the children
were asleep, Mary would take from their hiding place the
three handwrought boxes. And she and Joseph, holding
them in their hands, would wonder, and wondering,
would ask, "What does it all mean?"

Never did they touch the gold. Joseph's earnings sustained the family. And the gold was held in trust for the
coming maturity of him for whom it had been brought.

✦ ✦ ✦

Three years after Jesus' journey to Jerusalem, Joseph
died. Once again the family was in need. In the end it was
Numbidian who came to their aid.

The household labors were more than Mary could do in caring for James and Joses and Simon and the sisters and Jesus. But beyond that, food had to be bought, and no matter how carefully clothes were mended, finally they must be renewed.

Mary, who now depended completely upon her son Jesus, told him the secret of Numbidian's gift. "Use the gold, Mother," he urged, "as you see fit. It is really yours; it is not mine."

Numbidian's gold sustained the family over the years. And it was Mary who journeyed from Nazareth to the seacoast town of Caesarea, that there she might exchange the gold coins of Hyrcania for the currency of Palestine. Mary was uneasy as she saw the reserve grow less and less. But always her son reassured her: "Mother, it is as it should be."

Once, as she was preparing to go to Caesarea, she took a coin from the box, and as she turned, her hand struck the table and the coin fell. With the perversity of coins, it rolled crazily across the floor and out of sight. Mary swept the floor and searched the room with desperation, trying to find the coin she had lost.

That search gave Jesus a picture which he later told his followers. In the telling, the story was related, not in terms of a gold coin from Hyrcania, but in terms of pieces of silver: "What woman having ten pieces of silver, if she lose one piece, doth not light a candle, and sweep the house, and seek diligently until she find it?"

✦ ✦ ✦

Jesus, now grown into manhood, was still as he had always been—beyond Mary's complete understanding. The other children she knew. She could forecast what they would say and she could anticipate their needs. But his was a life that was different. He spoke about the God of Abraham and Isaac and Jacob with an intimacy that to her was almost frightening. He spoke with the same familiarity that he had used toward Joseph when Joseph was with them. He called God, "Father." Was that as it should be? She was never wholly sure. But always he gave her a sense that the affection of God surrounded her and sustained her. Constantly he said that that same surety about God was what his friends and neighbors and the people of his beloved land needed. "If only they knew," he said, "then they would live as children in their Father's world." And he was sure that his must be the task of bringing them thus to live.

+ + +

He told Mary his purpose. The day when he was to leave home was set. He was up and about before daybreak. But Mary had been sleepless all that night, wondering as only the mother of such a son would wonder. On the table, when he arose, he found food prepared by her hands so that he might eat before he left.

They stood in the doorway before the open door. He put his arm about her. "Mother, I shall always be in God's keeping. No matter what happens, will you know that I am doing his will? No harm can come to me or to you while we are in his hands."

In that hour she had no words. She fumbled for a moment in a little cloth bag. "Take this with you," she whispered. And she put into his hand a gold coin. It was the last of the gold coins that remained in Numbidian's box.

He took it. He embraced her. And he was gone. Never again did he sleep under her roof.

From that day to this he has been abroad among men. And wherever he has been, and wherever he is, there too is Numbidian, for Numbidian gave more than he knew!

THE
FOURTH WISE MAN'S
DETOUR

THE
FOURTH WISE MAN'S
DETOUR

BEHOLD, there came wise men from the east to Jerusalem"—so the telling of the Christmas story begins.

In the world of that day, wise-men–astrologers claimed to tell the influence of the stars on men's lives. At times rulers and kings were numbered among such wise men. None of these are known as widely as those who are linked with the birth of Jesus in the Gospel of Matthew. And we reach back in imagination to share their experience.

✦ ✦ ✦

In the late fall of the year of Jesus' birth, three wise-men–kings—whose names in ancient manuscripts now lost were Numbidian, Kelsorius, and Telfima—met together in the capital city of Ecbatana. Although publicly they had come to talk about forming political alliances, they had another concern: they were uneasy and wondering because of the recent appearance of a star in the east different from any they had ever seen.

Early in that year a Babylonian astrologer had discovered a papyrus dated at the time of the captivity of the Jewish people in Babylon. It contained a prophecy that a new star in the east would foretell the birth of one who was to be the universal ruler of all mankind. Numbidian had brought the papyrus with him.

The three kings read the prophecy with excitement. They sent a messenger to ask Zethar of Persia, another wise-man friend, to meet them in Ecbatana. As quickly as he could, Zethar joined them. They showed him the papyrus, telling him they were convinced that the new star pointed to the fulfillment of the prophecy.

Zethar examined the writing and concluded that the ascribed date was accurate and that it did come from a Hebrew writer. But he refused to believe that it provided any assurance or hope that in scorned, Roman-occupied Israel the future ruler of the world would be born. The prophecy, he said, had been concocted to bolster the hopes of the Jews in their exile. The fact that a star of increasing brilliance had appeared in the east was pure coincidence, and common sense suggested that the prophecy not be taken seriously. Zethar vehemently maintained that any notion that following the star would lead to the birthplace of the promised ruler was foolishness.

✦ ✦ ✦

Although Numbidian, Kelsorius, and Telfima respected Zethar as a man of independent and sound judgment, they themselves remained convinced of the accuracy of the prophecy telling of the star and of the universal ruler's birth.

After Zethar had left for his home in Persia, he learned

with incredulity that his friends had undertaken the journey following the star, despite his warnings.

✦ ✦ ✦

Weeks passed. Eventually the three kings returned to
the capital city of Ecbatana after having made their journey. Zethar, learning that they were on the way back,
went to meet them.

On that first chill evening, as the four men sat together
around the charcoal brazier, Zethar sensed that his friends
had curiously mingled and uncertain feelings about their
journey, on which they had evidently witnessed strange
happenings for which they had no satisfying explanation.

They described to Zethar how, after they had visited
Herod and paid their respects to him as ruler of the land,
they were led by the star to the hill village of Bethlehem;
and there, behind the inn, the star came to rest over a stable. In that stable they found a rough-handed carpenter
and a peasant girl, where earlier that night the girl had
given birth to her firstborn son. And in the stable, gathered around the little family, had been shepherds from
the nearby hills, telling of hearing singing—voices from
"on high" telling of the birth.

Zethar spoke with scorn. "What a spectacle! Seeking
the universal ruler to be born amid scenes of pageantry
and splendor, and finding a peasant family with a child in
a manger!"

But the journeying wise men did not and would not
agree that this was all they had found, nor would they
agree that this summed up the meaning of what they had
seen. They argued, with a conviction that Zethar could
not shake, that they had been in the presence of events

that had a meaning more than human. There *had* been voices and singing and music such as they had never heard in any eastern court; in the early-morning hours there had been light equal to the sun at noonday; there had been an illumination upon the faces of the mother and the child such as no mother and no son had ever shown before. And so overcome were they that they had been impelled to leave for the child the gifts that they had brought to present to the universal ruler—gold and frankincense and myrrh.

+ + +

But this was not all. Afterward they had had a dream which in its vividness had caused them to hasten home without returning to report their experiences to Herod. Warned in the dream, they returned by a seldom-traveled route. Near the northern border of Palestine, word reached them that Herod, in anger at their broken promise and deception and fearing a possible rival to his position and to Roman power, had ordered that all children two years of age and under be killed. And the sound of the wailing of the mothers of Israel for their children had followed the kings over their last hurried miles.

But they were sure that they had witnessed events on that memorable night beyond their understanding, beyond ordinary human events. They had no adequate explanation for their experience.

+ + +

Zethar remained unconvinced. "You and your stable king!—a puling infant! Imagine you on your knees in homage before a peasant's offspring, straw clinging to your garments . . . You!—you who share the wisdom of the ages and of the stars! How could you have been led into such foolery! How could you have been so duped?"

But Zethar's ridicule did not shake the confidence of the wise men that there had been more, much more, than the birth of a child to a peasant girl and a carpenter. The conclusion to which they came—and to which they held ever after—was that the gods have many ways of speaking to men, and why should they not speak quietly as well as with the voice of thunder? Why should they not speak through the humble as well as through the mighty?

✦ ✦ ✦

Always thereafter, in spite of his expressed doubts, the story told him by the wise men was the most disturbing fact in Zethar's life. He had known these men intimately —their judgment could not be lightly cast aside; they were not easily deceived. Reluctantly, Zethar came to feel that his friends had been in the presence of something which in his own heart he knew he would give his life to have seen.

For five years, day by day, Zethar pondered and wondered. There came a day when, without a word of intent or farewell, he left Persia and traveled toward Jerusalem, that there he might seek an answer to the question that was now at the center of his life: What was it that his friends had seen?

Zethar took with him to Jerusalem gold and treasure in abundance, such as any king in the eastern world would have envied.

✦ ✦ ✦

After Zethar reached Jerusalem, he settled in a house away from the main thoroughfares. For some months he moved about the city under the guise of being a Persian merchant's representative.

Zethar made inquiries quietly and with discretion. But no one seemed to have knowledge of the child's birth.

✦ ✦ ✦

Eventually, Zethar became friendly with an astrologer at the court of Herod's son and successor, Archelaus. One night when wine had loosened men's tongues, he ventured to ask this chief astrologer about Herod, and about the three wise men who had come to see him and who had returned home by another way.

"That, my friend," said the chief astrologer, "that is a story! Here were kings from other lands who told Herod that they were hoping to find the universal ruler shortly to be born in Israel. Never was a man more afraid than Herod. And," he continued, "the wise men must have found something, because they never came back. In his panic and anger, Herod ordered the slaughter of all young children under two years of age. He was never the same man after that. And for weeks on end he could not sleep, for his nights were filled with the sound of the wailing voices of sorrowing mothers.

"All we could ever find out was that there had been a bright light over the hills of Bethlehem; and some of the people nearby said that they had been wakened at night by the sound of singing voices, but they did not know what it meant. My guess is that a comet flashed across the skies and simple people gave rein to their imaginations."

And then realizing that he had talked about a forbid-

den subject, the astrologer stopped abruptly. "Never—
never say to anyone that I have spoken to you about
Herod and the kings and the events of that night."

✦ ✦ ✦

On the next day Zethar, taking with him but one servant, rode out to the village of Bethlehem and stopped at
the Bethlehem Inn, owned by Simon. Zethar told Simon
that he was from Persia; that he had been staying in Jerusalem on business, but needed the quiet of village life for
a time because he was weary and tired.

As the days passed, he and Simon found companionship
together, and they began to relate to each other the sights
and wonders which they had seen on their travels in different parts of the world. Once, near the end of a long
evening of conversation, Simon said: "But I have seen
amazing wonders in this very village. Nothing in my life
has perplexed me as much as something that took place
behind my own inn six years ago."

Zethar's breathing quickened as he said, "Exciting
events could never come to this little village among the
hills!"

Simon answered: "Six years ago it seemed that the gods
had found this place and for a brief hour had looked
down upon it with the light of their presence. You may
not believe it, but in that stable across the courtyard,
amid scenes of celestial brilliance, strange events such as
I have not understood took place. There—there was born
a child to a peasant girl and a carpenter; a star stood over
the stable; light filled the heavens; there were singing
voices; kings from afar came with rich gifts. But more
than all these, there was something about the child, some-

121

thing about the mother, that was not of this earth."

And Zethar tried to ask calmly: "What about it?—What happened—then?"

Simon answered: "The child and the parents fled to Egypt, warned in a dream to escape Herod's wrath. And the dream was true because hardly had they gotten away from the village when Herod's soldiers, under orders, gathered up all the young children and killed them. Somehow, Herod knew something about this birth and he was afraid that it threatened his power. But the child's parents, warned by that dream, had fled—luckily—to Egypt!"

"They went to Egypt?" queried Zethar. "That was a strange journey to make! Which way did they go?"

"By a seldom-used route." Simon took down a map and spread it on the floor. He pointed out the direction he had suggested to them. "They planned to go this way," he said.

✦ ✦ ✦

With barely the courtesy of a farewell to Simon, Zethar returned to Jerusalem, gathered supplies, and with his servants set out to follow the route to Egypt shown him by Simon the innkeeper.

Zethar never found answers to his inquiries. In the first Egyptian village to which they came, no one there knew; they made their way to Pelusium—no one there knew; they made their way to Alexandria—no one there knew. In the towns and cities of Egypt to which they traveled for months and years, there were no answers—no one knew.

In despair Zethar returned to Jerusalem.

122

In Jerusalem he became a familiar figure as he wandered about the streets, as he studied the stars by night, as he accumulated old Hebrew manuscripts. He became expert in Hebrew language and customs. He studied the writings and prophecies that told of the Messiah that was to come. So assiduously did he search, so eagerly did he question, that he became known as "the mad astrologer."

+ + +

Years passed. Jerusalem and the nearby countryside were gossiping and excited about a new prophet, a teacher, a healer, quite outside the orthodox circles of Jewish religious life—one Jesus of Nazareth. His sayings circulated among the people, sayings very different from the exhortations of the priests and scribes and Pharisees of the day:

"If ye love them which love you, what reward have ye?"

"The Sabbath was made for man, and not man for the Sabbath."

"Blessed are the peacemakers."

"Lay not up for yourselves treasures upon earth."

The religious authorities hated him; the common people heard him gladly.

There was evidence that the healing powers of the gods were in his hands. It was even said that he had raised the dead.

Zethar had heard the young teacher. And questions began to haunt his waking hours: Whence came this Jesus? Where did this teacher grow up? What was his background? How did he come to have this wisdom?

One day he overheard someone call the teacher "Jesus

of Nazareth." And to Nazareth Zethar went. There he was directed to the house where Mary lived. Mary, with a mother's assurance and pride, told Zethar of the greatness of her son. And because she felt the yearning interest of Zethar in her son, she related the circumstances of his birth in Bethlehem. Then, from a compartment in her kitchen cupboard, she brought out the bejewelled leather box that had contained Numbidian's gold—the gold he had left as a gift for the child in the manger. Zethar grasped the box when he recognized on it the embossed royal symbol of Numbidian's kingdom. At last he had found the answer to his lifelong quest! Now he must go back to the man himself.

✦ ✦ ✦

But the sands were running low in Zethar's hourglass of life. With almost the last of the money that remained of the great treasure that he had once brought from Persia, Zethar bought a tomb in a garden. It was a tomb wherein no man's body had ever been laid. As weary day followed weary day, he tried to fit together the pieces of the puzzle of his life.

✦ ✦ ✦

The time of the Passover drew near. All Jerusalem was seething with rumors and threats that gathered around Jesus' presence in the city.

There came Jesus' arrest and trial. The news of his condemnation ran from one end of the city to the other.

Zethar, leaning heavily on his servant's arm, was among those who followed the crowd outside the city to the hill

124

of Calvary. As he looked upon the man in whom he had found a wisdom about life more profound than he had ever known before, the man of whose birth the woman Mary had told him, the man whom his three friends had seen as a newborn child—as he saw the spirit in which Jesus came to his death, Zethar said to himself: Thirty-three years ago my friends were right and I was wrong. This man is in truth the Messiah.

✦ ✦ ✦

In Jerusalem, Zethar had become acquainted with Joseph of Arimathea—a secret follower of the carpenter-teacher. That tragic evening of the crucifixion, Zethar and his servant, entering Joseph of Arimathea's home, found him racked by sobs, weeping because of the death of Jesus, whom he had loved more dearly than his own life. Zethar, putting his hand on Joseph's shoulder, said: "Joseph, use my tomb in the garden so that there his body may find a resting-place. For I call him, even as did the centurion, the Son of God."

And the body of the man whom Zethar's friends had seen as the babe of Bethlehem was laid to rest in Zethar's tomb.

✦ ✦ ✦

The strange, perplexing, triumphant events of the resurrection followed. And Zethar knew, beyond any doubt, that he, Zethar, for whom the star had never shone, had met and seen and heard the Messiah, not as a babe, but as a man—and more than man—with the hand of God's favor upon him.

And now Zethar was at peace—the first peace he had known for thirty-three years. And on his lips was the prayer: "Lord, now let your servant depart in peace, for I have seen, and I know, and I believe."

✦ ✦ ✦

Finally, the body of Zethar rested in his own, now-empty tomb in the garden. And Zethar's servant always said that as Zethar went to his reward, he heard a voice, "Enter thou into the joy of thy Lord."